I0590978

Spirituality and the Relational in a Trilogy.

Meeting Emma
The Primacy of Love
The Language of Love.

Three modern stories about the love of God and
people. It offers insights on many topics and freshens
up the Christian faith. Some ideas are new, others simply
important. Do care to be different - read and reflect.
Theology can be fun!

Each book is an independent read.

The Language of Love

Authenticity and the True Self

Michael J Spyker

AgapeDeum

Published in Adelaide, Australia by AgapeDeum
Contact: agapedeum.com

ISBN 978-0-6486957-6-9

Copyright © Michael J Spyker 2017

All right reserved. Other than for the purpose and subject to the conditions prescribed under the *Copyright Act*, no part of this publication may be reproduced, stored in a retrieval system, or transmitted in any form or by any means, electronic, mechanical, photocopying, recording and otherwise, without prior permission of the publisher.

This edition published in 2020

Publication assistance by Immortalise
Cover design: Ben Morton

The places mentioned in this story are real but every character is fictitious.

Preface

In *The Language of Love* Emma and Jake fall in love. It raises important questions. About their relationship and modern society. About the power of love in general. How about Eros for instance, what is that all about? Here, I have been guided by Rollo May's *Love and Will* and *Love & Friendship* by Allan Bloom.

The Language of Love is a human adventure. Emma and Jake are grappling with their emotions in discovering love, while making their way camping into the fabulous Flinders Ranges in South Australia in search of a friend.

The Language of Love discusses Gospel relevancy and the relational in philosophy also.

PART ONE

1

A BIRD WAS SINGING beautifully in short bursts beyond the open window when Emma woke up slowly into a new day. She listened for a while. It was early light and the street front was still quiet. Emma let the birdsong happen to her and enjoyed it. The house she lived in was quiet too. But the quiet had an empty feel. The room across the passage way, now unoccupied, had become a bother.

Ruth, her housemate and friend of university days, was sleeping next door. Last night they had chewed the cud and drank a bottle of red. He'll be fine, Ruth had insisted feigning little interest. He's capable and, after all, on holidays. Who knows when he'll be back?

True enough, but not convincing, not to Emma. She figured that those holidays were stretching on longer than ever intended. JH should be back in his room by now. Admittedly, he was a traveller by nature, a nomad of sorts. But something might have happened, a kind of mishap perhaps. JH didn't have relatives in Australia nor real friends, as far as Emma knew – no one to take much interest.

Should she have a holiday herself? On that question she had fallen asleep last night. A search for JH would make for an excellent excuse. She could do with a break from city life having grown up amongst the farms.

Emma knew where JH was headed: north towards the wild country. That's what he had told them. Finding him there, in such a large area, would be a challenge. But the roads were few and tourist destinations limited. He was bound to visit some of those. Many places of interest were off the beaten track though. No matter how well you prepared, the outback could spring its surprises. And JH might not be outback savvy – she couldn't be sure. Admittedly, South America had plenty of open country as well. JH came from there.

It would be unwise to take on a search alone, Emma knew. Unforeseen events were always possible and best faced together with a friend. She would ask Jake along but explain that they might be chasing a false alarm. He would come. That thought ran a tingle down her spine. Out, amongst the majestic mountains of the Northern Flinders with Jake. It had a primal feel to it, a tempting of fate. Emma smiled faintly. She could do with a bit of adventure. Since that one day months ago, when both JH and Jake had walked into the pub where she worked the bar, much had changed for her.

The sound of traffic was now filling Emma's room. It was time to have a shower. JH needed finding. Simply, that's how she felt. It was a good excuse for a holiday also. Decision made, she rolled out of bed.

2

IT HAD BEEN MID AFTERNOON on a hot day in late January. The street was like an oven and the tables on the pavement outside the pub where Emma worked remained empty. The East end of Adelaide felt deserted with few cars travelling through. Pedestrians were scarce, but that would improve nearing dinner time.

Emma worked the lunch and afternoon shift that day at the front bar, where it was cool enough. Every summer had its hot spells, with many yet to come in the months ahead. Business places were equipped to handle it. Today's heat, plus the fact that many people had spent their cash on Christmas and the holiday season, meant that the number of punters was low. A few hard core regulars sat with their backs against the far end of the bar gazing at the overhead TV in the corner. Possibly, they didn't have much cooling at home and counted on pubs or shopping centres to find comfort. Only a skeleton staff had been called in with Emma, as a better worker, enjoying preference. She could do with the money, no question.

The pub was an old one, renovated to a point. Its history remained noticeable in some timbers and the ornate ceiling. Plus the wooden main door with a vintage logo on its glass window. Emma was checking stock levels of spirits against the wall behind the bar when that door opened. A man of medium height walked in. He was wearing a wide-rimmed hat over black hair. His face had an olive reddish tinge. Most likely a tourist of some sort, Emma thought, though the hat reminded her of the outback. His bearing was upright and unassuming. He looked around with interest, moved towards the bar, and took a seat. Upon closer scrutiny Emma noticed a scar across his left cheek. Obviously the wound had never seen plastic surgery. In his mid-thirties, she figured, and handsome. He smiled at her.

'What's a popular beer here?' The smile lit up his face.

'Local one: it's Coopers Pale,' Emma replied.

'One of those, please.'

'How large would you like, a schooner or a pint?'

'The biggest, please.'

She skilfully drew a pint of Coopers and placed it in front of the man, who handed her a ten dollar note. Immediately, the cold glass drew moisture from the air and a wet sheen settled over it. Emma handed the change back without a word and walked away a little. Don't bother customers unless asked and then respond speedily. It was an important rule behind the bar. One of the TV watchers drew her attention a few moments later.

Another rule was to ask a customer if all was okay, after a while. Whether anything else would be needed, like a bite to eat. It might make an extra sale. The mention of food seemed to tickle hunger or nibble pains.

'I could do with a sandwich,' the man admitted. 'Chicken salad, something like that.'

'Would you like it normal or spicy?' Emma asked.

'Hot spicy.' He smiled again, his brown eyes friendly and intelligent.

Emma scribbled a note for the kitchen and hit a button. The note would be picked up by a kitchen hand. Why didn't it surprise her that the man had asked for very spicy. Because he looks kind of Mexican, she thought.

Another regular walked in through the side door that led to the toilets and joined her at the counter. She didn't like the guy because he always looked at her chest overly long. Emma had become quite used to having her figure scrutinised. It was par for the course when serving behind a bar and mostly an innocuous happening. It was best not to imagine how the punters processed their images of the pretty barmaid. It would be a pointless and unnecessary exercise. But with this guy and his seedy eyes it was different. She felt like giving him a tongue lashing, but of course didn't. Before she could serve him, the chicken sandwich arrived to which she attended first. Next she planted the drink she knew the regular wanted in front of him and took the twenty he had placed on the counter. She replaced it with his change; then got back to stocktaking with her back to the customers.

The stranger had an interesting face, Emma concluded. He had accepted the sandwich gracefully giving her just the right attention to convey a sense of respect. He seemed to disapprove of the seedy regular. While saying a kind thank you for the sandwich their eyes had met briefly. It was a face she wouldn't mind painting, Emma thought. Though faces weren't her preference. That was streets, buildings and architecture. She had seen plenty of those, significant ones too, while travelling through Europe about a year ago. Hundreds of pictures she had taken with a proper camera instead of her phone. Her aunt, who was a well-known painter, had financed the trip as a reward for finishing an art degree at university. Now back in Adelaide, Emma was facing the budding artist's problem of making a living while pursuing her passion. It meant serving in a pub. Fortunately one of the better ones, with a management who treated the staff okay. It could be different, and had been at her previous place of work.

Though giving the appearance of being busy, she needed to remain attentive to her customers. When the stranger had finished his beer Emma walked over purposefully taking the empty glass and asked whether a replacement was needed. Yes, but a smaller size, was the reply. Emma poured a schooner. After a fresh drink had been set before him the man spoke.

'Could I ask you a question, Emma?'

Her name was embroidered on her work T-shirt, supplied by the company with a purposefully tight fit. She didn't mind him addressing her personally.

'Sure.'

The man had a nice voice and might be a good

singer; perhaps was.

'I'm planning to stay in town for a while and need to find a room. You're local. What's the best way of going about that?' He looked at her expectantly.

The question took Emma aback. She saw a hand go up at the other end of the bar requesting service and excused herself for a moment telling she would be back in a sec. It was a welcome interruption for suddenly Emma had to make a decision, a rather important one. Serving gave her a few seconds to think the matter over. After pulling another beer for one of the TV watchers she returned to the stranger, her mind sort of made up.

'Sorry,' she apologised, which was waived away.

'You mean a room like lodging or house sharing?' Emma wondered.

'Yes, preferably sharing. Need be nothing special. But clean, not trashed out.'

'What cost do you have in mind?' The question gave Emma further time to think and decide.

'Not much of an issue, but not exorbitant.' The man looked at her with interest sensing that somehow his request received more attention than he had expected.

'I may know of a room,' Emma admitted. 'Rather, I do know of a room, but I'm not the only one to decide.'

She mulled things over for a moment.

The man waited patiently.

Emma was house sharing with her friend Ruth of late. Just recently, a month before Christmas, they had moved into a three bedroom place together that was perfect but pricey – not for the area it was in, but for their budget. It would be best if a third occupant could be found. Not just anyone - that was the problem. A house with friction they could do without. Three girls together could be a problem, potentially. Perhaps a guy would be a better idea. Between them they could handle that easily. But, of course, not any sort of guy. They had decided to wait and see. Now she was facing this stranger, had little idea of what he was like, and needed to give an answer about a room being available. The house had an annex that could be offered as a separate living space. Her gut feeling was that he'd be alright. Ruth needed to agree, of course, and that was a way out. If she didn't, the third bedroom room would stay empty.

'There is a room at my place,' Emma said. 'But my friend Ruth needs to agree.'

'Sure.' The man smiled and did not press the issue, let matters take their course.

'Phone me later today, after 6. Ruth will be home by then. If she agrees to meet you I will give you the address. It's not far from here.'

Emma wrote her number on the food ordering pad and tore it off. When she handed it to him she realised she had no idea of the stranger's name and asked for it.

'Thank you,' he said accepting the slip of paper. 'My name is Jesus – Jesus Hombrenos.'

He pronounced his first name the Spanish way, but Emma understood it well enough. Not many in Australia were called Jesus, not like where he came from.

Soon after the stranger had left the door swung open and a man close to her own age walked in. It gave her a jolt of recognition. Some weeks ago they had chatted at an art exhibition where she was supervising for a few hours. A number of her paintings were on display. Twice every year a local art group put on a show and Emma was part of that. On his way out he had started a brief conversation asking whether she was an artist herself perhaps and why that was so. What would you say to that in a few seconds? Something like, I always wanted to be – though obviously there was much more to it than that. But he had been rather nice and now unexpectedly appeared in the pub – tall, with blond hair and very blue eyes. You could tell he was clever. The way he looked about him unobtrusively; seemed to take things in, giving it attention. Their brief talk had been a little unnerving, actually. Not that he had meant it so. Man number two today, Emma thought, who is interesting but I don't know his name. They had never got that familiar. This turned out to be quite an afternoon, here in the pub. Life was full of surprises. She tried not to show that she recognised him.

'I found you,' he said.

'You did,' Emma confirmed, a little surprised. She had not imagined that he might be looking for her.

'Lucky me,' he smiled.

'Perhaps.' Emma had no idea whether he would be lucky, not as yet. 'What would you like – to drink?' She emphasised the last words slightly and rebuked herself. Her defensive pub persona could come to the fore a little too quickly at times.

'Sorry.' He seemed to mean it. 'A schooner please, of Coopers Pale.'

Soon it was placed before him. Emma should have walked away but hesitated.

'Don't tell me I have been completely erased from your memory,' he said.

That's not the way in which Emma would have put it. Nor anyone else she knew. The guy had a way with words, sounded educated. She found it attractive though. A bit like an artist with language he seemed to be, a writer perhaps.

'Not quite,' she admitted. 'How did you find me then?' She couldn't help asking. No-one required her attention, so she could have a chat.

'I was here last weekend when the live music was on, in the beer garden, and saw you working the bar.'

That was true enough. It had been a busy night, so many customers. Emma had not noticed him.

'But how did you know I would be here today?'

'I didn't, just took a punt. I've just come from Adelaide Uni and could do with a drink. Decided to come by.'

'You're a student?' Emma ventured. It seemed not quite right.

'Used to be. Just visited the library.' He had placed a linen bag on the stool next to him. Must be for books, Emma concluded.

New customers walked in, a couple in fact. She attended to their requests leaving the guy with his beer. Giving him a sideway glance later on he seemed to have drifted off into thought, completely at ease. Emma was intrigued. She had never met someone like him. At least it felt that way. Having executed her duties she returned to continue their conversation deciding not to beat about the bush.

'Why were you looking for me?' she asked, having a good idea why.

'Because I would have kicked myself, if I hadn't.' He lifted his eyebrows and gave a shrug of the shoulders. Indicating: that's how it is.

Emma smiled. 'And that would have hurt,' she said. This talk was turning out okay, definitely different.

'Yeah. In my gut,' he explained. 'An emotional hurt.'

He also smiled, at this attractive girl with her short dark hair. She had hung around in his thoughts a lot lately. Last weekend it had been impossible and unwise to attract her attention. She being busy and the place packed with noise and people. Today, his luck had changed, hopefully. But he should stop this talk about kicking and hurting, be more conventional.

'So you're asking me not to hurt you?' Listen to yourself, Emma thought. But this conversation was fun and the guy interesting.

'Please not,' he said with a brief grin, encouraged by the response for it was tongue in cheek. 'I went back to the exhibition the next day, but you weren't there. The man in charge had no idea where you could be contacted. Then I found you in this pub.'

Emma took this information without comment. She was used to guys seeking her out, but preferred the company of her girlfriends – less complicated. Still, she liked interesting people, males not excluded. You had to avoid becoming overly careful in life and you miss your opportunities. Was one staring her in the face? There was only one way to find out. Commit, girl, she told herself. You too might kick yourself, if you don't. All this flashed through her mind in seconds.

'So, what now?' she asked.

This direct question made him gather his thoughts. His face opened up with a shade of relief for obviously Emma's was a leading question.

'Lunch, dinner, nightclub, you name it?'

The words hung in the air finding no immediate response. Not quite as self-assured as he makes out to be, Emma thought. She liked it all the better.

'I don't even know your name,' she said. 'You would have figured that I am Emma.'

'Sorry, I should have mentioned it. My name is Jake.'

For the second time that day Emma scribbled her phone number on the ordering pad. She handed it to Jake. 'Call me,' she said, moving away to attend to a customer. When Jake left she gave him a brief wave. What a day. Two new men in her life in one afternoon, Jesus and Jake. Was this a joke, perhaps? She didn't think so.

3

BUSHES AND WATTLES and the occasional gum tree lining the road flashed by. At one stretch a fire had gone through, undoubtedly during summer when anything that created sufficient heat could ignite the dry land. Lightning strikes or a piece of glass, whatever. That would not be a problem today, Jake thought. It was July and winter. He was looking lazily out of the window, still waking up. They had not long ago left Blyth. Emma was driving.

Quite a localised fire, Jake mused, but intense. The damage was obvious to the eye. He knew that wattles, a hardy small tree, always survived best. Heat helped germinate their seed. Not so with gums. They could smoulder deeply into their root system for days and might die. When a gum survived, but its crown got burned, it would begin to have fresh leaves appearing directly on the trunk and branches. Dashes of bright green against sooty coloured bark. Those new leaves were drawing moisture from the soil. Increasingly so as their number grew. It was the start of the restoration process. Most of the burned gums Jake saw that morning remained lifeless. They were fairly young trees and part of a revegetation exercise.

The car moved along speedily through farm country and would do for many miles to come. Traffic was sparse. The hills were covered with crops, still green, for harvest was yet months away. Closer to the mountains in the far north it would be sheep and cattle country. The soil was too barren for a crop and the weather potentially extreme. Tonight they would set up camp in those mountains. Jake could never be a farmer. The benefits were unpredictable and the struggles substantial. He liked the wide outdoors, but not like that.

On the horizon in the west a wind farm could be seen. It connected to the electricity grid between Port Augusta and Adelaide. Faintly it was turning its massive blades. An impressive sight, if you liked that kind of thing. How far the wind farm stretched and how many towers it counted, Jake didn't know. The grid was hundreds of miles long. More towers had been planned.

'Look,' Emma said, 'a wedgy.' A wedge-tail eagle was hovering against the wind making every effort to remain in one spot while seeking prey below. 'I once knew of a nest and kept observing it off and on for days. If only I could fly, I thought.'

'Got it,' Jake confirmed. The large bird was near the road and easily spotted. They soon passed it by.

'I don't think, I had started high school yet.' Emma sounded as if she had lost something.

She probably has, Jake thought – the wonder and spontaneity of childhood.

Two days ago he had been living blissfully in the city when Emma phoned. I need your help, Jake. Of course, she could count on that. That he would be going up north, on some kind of holiday with a purpose, had been a complete surprise. Not a bad one either, the idea of spending time with Emma in the outback.

The open country had grown on him during his adventure a few years ago. With Baz, his godfather, he had taken on the thousand sand hills of the Simpson Desert. Miles of red sand and starry nights. It was a trip he would never forget. The beauty of the desert and their talks about the ideas of Liam. Jake had been sixteen when his farther Liam was killed in an accident.

He would not have heard the thoughts of his father about the centrality of love and the relational, if it weren't for Baz. Jake had not visited the outback since. Circumstances and the lack of equipment, particularly a four-wheel drive vehicle, had prevented it.

Baz had hinted once that he would be welcome on another trip. Jake had declined, not feeling the need for a surrogate father. Of course, that wasn't Baz's intention. Jake figured that somehow he had understood though. When Baz was approached about the borrowing of a swag plus a cold weather sleeping bag, it was offered with pleasure. To the Northern Flinders, Jake had explained, with Emma. Baz hadn't queried it. He was good like that, left people to live their lives freely. That they would be looking for JH remained unmentioned for Jake had been in a hurry. By nature he wasn't the most informative person anyway. Kept to himself. Unless discussing ideas that were of interest. Then he could talk all night.

He had met JH in Emma's kitchen. It was the night of their first date. Emma, not quite ready, had ushered Jake in and introduced him. JH shook a firm hand and smiled. He was boiling water for a cup of tea and asked if Jake would like one. Please do, Emma had said. It gave her time to get ready. The day had been busier than expected – nothing unusual in that.

Only later did Jake discover that JH's full name was Jesus Hombrenos. Ruth and Emma preferred calling him JH, even though they could say his name in Spanish easily. Jesus began to introduce himself as JH to others from then on. It sounded properly Australian.

Even now, months later, Jake didn't really know him that well. Nor did Emma, he imagined. JH was surely intelligent, always kind, and great to talk to. But he never told much about himself, only occasionally. And yet, somehow he was known, without being known well. The essential nature of the man was not in question. He was a fine person, someone who grew on you. That would be why Emma was so adamant that they should try finding him. Perhaps she felt a kind of loss, rather than really being worried about his disappearance. Jake could not be sure, nor did it matter. He was more than happy to join the search.

Over their cup of tea they had made small talk. JH explained that he came from South America and visited Australia to see what it was like. Adelaide appealed to him as it was a smaller city. Not all that far from the bush either, which he would like to visit one day. Still, far enough, Jake explained, but relatively close by

Australian standards. JH shrugged and gave the impression that distances wouldn't bother him. Before Jake could tell about his own background, Emma appeared.

'Your car, or mine?' she asked.

With Emma working in the city, Jake suggested drive to Henley Beach instead. He had borrowed his mother's car, not having or needing one of his own. Living at home had its advantages. Some years ago faced with the option of leaving he had decided to remain with his mum, who was alone. One day that was bound to change.

'Henley Beach is fine,' Emma agreed. She could do with a bit of sea air. 'And, before you drive off, let's agree to pay half each of the bill.'

Jake had come prepared to cover the full cost and glanced sideways at his companion. She looked simply stunning; stunning in a simple way.

'Otherwise, I'm not coming,' Emma grinned.

'Okay. We're going Dutch,' Jake agreed. 'I won't let you slip away that easily.'

Emma had no intention of slipping away. She had been looking forward to this date. Something about Jake was very attractive and not just his good looks. But it was early days with disappointment always a possibility.

They found a restaurant near the beach. Behind the sand dunes next to a small square that was an entry point to the sea. Being a warm evening with the seafront offering a cooling breeze, the area was busy. They took a table outdoors shaded from the sun. Which soon was to set, bathing the whole coast in indirect light. Already the sky at the horizon had a reddish tinge that would change into a full blooded glow until the orange ball in the sky was down. Adelaide, on the eastern side of a large bay, was known for its sunsets. Perfect, Emma concluded, giving it her artist's eye.

Their talk was typically that of two people finding their way. When the food arrived it became easier – something else to focus on. Emma was happy, but not quite. Jake felt okay, but he was struggling. Small-talk wasn't his strong suit. Let's delve in a bit deeper, Emma decided. See what there is to be found. Plenty, she felt. With the intuition of someone who tried to look past first impressions. That was important with art, seeing in ways others might not.

'What makes you tick, Jake?' she asked.

He looked at her inquiringly. Saw both interest and a challenge. Emma was not a superficial companion, Jake understood. He felt all the better for it. Slowly a smile broke out on his face. 'If you really want to know,

I'll tell you,' he said.

'I do.' Emma was wondering what was to come. Jake sounded kind of apologetic.

'My main interest is philosophy,' Jake told her. As a mathematician he would be ideally suited to analytic philosophy, but that wasn't his focus. It was people and society. His father's ideas left a deep impression on him. He was trying to work those out further with a different approach.

'I have no idea about that,' Emma admitted. 'It must be interesting.'

'It is. If you have a mind for it. Many people consider it a waste of time.'

'Many people consider art a waste of time as well,' Emma responded.

'Point taken.'

Brothers-in-arms they were. Jake found it a pleasant sensation. He worked with ideas and Emma with images. She used paints and he used words. They were both looking for understanding in their particular way.

'Philosophy aims at finding truth about how things really are. That means speculation and a great number of ideas. For thousands of years those have been gathered, looking at matters from all angles. You must be interested in ideas about life and people and the universe, for philosophy to appeal to you. At times, those ideas can be quite influential. You would have heard of Karl Marx and communism, for instance.' Or Nietzsche and Hitler's adaptation, Jake could have added.

'And you have some of those ideas yourself?' Emma surmised, ignoring the comment about Marx. She felt, Jake was unlikely to stick with what had already been written – just an impression.

'Yes. Or rather, I have the one prominent Idea. A focus is always needed to give philosophy cohesion.'

Emma sipped her wine. 'Go on, then,' she said.

'The philosopher is convinced of the validity of that Idea and will try to explain how it connects with everyday life. Certain ideas, like mine, can be both practical and philosophical.'

'So you have an idea, you explain it, and live by it,' Emma summed it up.

'Well, yes. You may try to approximate it. The Idea itself is larger than a person can express. The challenge is to explain the Idea adequately, to construct a framework of reasoning. One that accommodates the many aspects of life that are associated with the Idea.'

Emma had followed that quite well and asked the obvious question. 'And you have such an Idea?'

'Yes, I do. I have learned from my father that everything essentially is relational. He explained that from a mostly theological perspective. I will take an existential approach. What does life look like, if relation is the benchmark? That's not a new question, of course. Relation, usually in the form of relationality, is a popular topic in our society, but not really in modern philosophy.'

'Your father is a theologian?' Emma had noted that Jake spoke of him in the past tense but decided to ignore it. Just to be sure.

'Used to be – he died in an accident.'

She gave that a nod of the head. Her own father was alive and well, but hardly ever home sailing the seven seas for a job. It no longer annoyed her.

'So what about relationality – what have you found?' Beyond interacting with friends or family, what could be said about it? Plenty, it seemed.

Jake gave her a measured look. It would be best if their discussion avoided too much philosophical detail.

'Try me.' Emma spoke with a little steel in her voice. She perceived Jake's hesitation and guessed the reason for it. Thought it a little condescending. She was sensitive like that, always had been.

'Okay. Thanks.' Jake was beginning to figure what

this gorgeous girl was really about. It was stirring his emotions. 'I'll gladly tell you.'

He took his glass, twirled the red wine about, took a sip, and continued.

'Just an outline. That will do for now, and I haven't got that far with it yet.'

Slowly he placed the glass back on the table.

'To me there are three basic aspects of the relational. There is *general* being – all simply exists in relation – everything, the universe, the world, people, nature, you name it. Then, focusing on people – though to anything that has consciousness it would be relevant – there is *inner* being. That also is relationally determined, but different from general being. Thirdly, there is *functional* being. It concerns the relational in our actions. I am particularly interested in inner and functional being in reference to people and modern society.'

Well, she'd asked for that, Emma thought. It seemed interesting though. I'm on my way to being smitten, she realised. But it was early days.

'Inner being concerns my deepest emotions. My raison d'être you could say. While the functional is the expression of my being. But what do those realities mean? How does it make me the person I am, help make a better one? Much has been written about that particularly in psychology, of course. I will address it philosophically. Not doing experiments, but as theory. By reflection based on my reading and existential observations. Perhaps I can add a little to understanding what being human means. And, I will aim for simplicity.'

Even to Jake's own ears it sounded a little fanciful.

Emma perceived his hesitation, one she was familiar with. Would she really ever manage that painting with distinctly her own style? She wasn't sure, but definitely would try. The very question touched on how life was best lived, on human potential.

'And you will make that Idea important in your life?' Emma remembered the third point of Jake's explanation, about him as a philosopher.

'I will work at it.' It sounded not that convincing. More like a declaration of good intentions.

At least, he is honest, Emma thought. And a little careful about things. She understood that Jake was setting himself up for a challenge, getting the relational right – in practice. Funny, but she had been thinking about that herself lately. The importance of the relational.

They were approaching Laura. A pretty small town

taking pride in counting the poet C.J. Dennis, who wrote *The Sentimental Bloke*, as one of its residents during his youth. In the late eighteen hundreds. The median strip featured pepper trees and the sidewalks likewise. There was considerable vegetation. Old style shops on either side shaped the main street. Quite a few were for sale, some of them empty. It was the nature of modern country living. The big supermarkets and major stores in much larger towns were no more than half an hour away.

'I have an aunt here, on a farm,' Emma said. 'Last year there was a massive fire over the range, which you can see on your left. It is inaccessible country with many valleys that hadn't burned for a hundred years. The fire was frightening. It lit up the sky for many days. It was visible for miles around, even as far as Peterborough. A forest further north fully burned out. It included a long abandoned trial nursery from over a century ago with trees from all over the world. There they decided on Radiata pine as the best building timber for our country. Those trees thrive in Australia.'

Emma was a mine of information, Jake thought. But then, she had grown up in this region.

'This town might have been evacuated had it not been for the fire breaks they bulldozed, water bombing aircrafts, and a wind change. I saw a picture of the farmers and their small vehicles helping the fire brigade. They carried a pump and water tank. It was like a colony of ants crawling up the hillside. Everyone worked till exhaustion.'

'Was your aunt okay?'

'Yes. They needed to replace some fences. The fire encroached onto their property. It was a close call.'

At the Laura caravan park they turned right, direction Orroroo.

4

EMMA ENJOYED DRIVING the road to Orroroo once past Appila. The hills became steeper and the valleys deeper. At some stretches you could see for miles, at others not. It was beautiful country. Yesterday, they had left Adelaide for her parents' place. Near a small town called Blythe. They lived on a few acres just off the road to Clare, one of the major wine areas of South Australia in the north. It was not where Emma had grown up though. Her dad had insisted on moving not that long ago. Mum complaining it would make her lose too many friends. They won't be that far away, he had argued, but missed the point. They would be too far for a frequent visit. Still, it had become increasingly difficult to manage the farm with dad hardly ever around. The farmer who had leased their land purchased it. Mum could see the benefits of a shift closer to "the city", as Adelaide was often called. Country life was rather isolating, whatever your view of it. Emma had mentioned that a place near Clare would make visiting home easier for her. But will you come, Emma? Her mother knew all about good intentions.

Briefly she glanced sideways at Jake who appeared deep in thought. He seemed to enter that kind of state easily. Emma had no idea whether this was normative to having philosophy as an interest. She didn't mind and could appreciate what reflection might offer. Surely in the quiet, if you could find that somewhere. It reminded her of Joe, a friend older than her father. She should have a coffee with him one day soon. She hadn't been in touch for ages.

Joe had introduced her to ideas like meditation, contemplation and all kinds that related to Christian spirituality. Much you could give a try. Just see what appeals to you, he had encouraged her. At least you now know about it. It was true. Before their talks she had no idea of the richness of the Christian tradition. To date she had kept the need for detachment in mind and reflective prayer. Meeting Joe had been a good thing. Not just because of what he had told her, but also his help during a time that had been difficult. When a good friend died in a fatal car accident. Country roads can be a killer, Emma thought. Especially when you're young.

She had left for Europe and lost contact with Joe. That needed to change, Emma decided.

She had loved her European vacation. Every country was brimming with culture and proper history. Not like the 200 plus years of Australia, though that was interesting too. All that art from Rome, to Paris, to Amsterdam. It had been completely overwhelming. An overdose of what she loved most: of beauty. Deep inside she felt a thirst that would never be quenched. One that lasted a lifetime. She couldn't really explain it, but simply knew it to be so.

The general notion was that beauty depended on the eye of the beholder and to an extent that was true. That kind of beauty you could handle in small quantities, take ownership of in some way. But real beauty, beauty at large, was simply uncontainable. So much bigger than a solitary human being could ever handle. It was like a mine that needed digging to find nuggets of gold. You needed to strike your pick, see what would happen, and strike again. As soon as you took a rest, as of course you would, the mundane took over. The sensations of ordinary life.

Emma remembered her first date with Jake when she had asked him about what made him tick. Of course, he had asked her likewise. She would not normally have answered that with the passion she felt. Usually people considered art mostly interesting. They didn't get it. Jake was different though, as his talk about philosophy bore out. When she declared beauty as her main interest, he had called her a romantic. Misunderstanding, she had strongly objected. Poor Jake, he had scrambled for cover. At pains to explain that he was referring to a movement in philosophy called the Romantics. It placed great store in the importance of beauty. The time of the Renaissance, he had said, in the days of Rousseau.

Emma had not immediately responded.

A recognition of the importance of beauty in life dates from way back to Plato, much before the days of Christ. And Plotinus, not long after, she was told.

Jake had looked a little desperate. At least, you are trying to understand, she had said with a smile. Emma normally didn't give a great deal about whether someone did. She just knew what she felt in her gut. Still, being taken seriously was nice. And now she was facing another kind of beauty. She was in love, no two ways about that. But hadn't declared her hand yet, beyond kissing. In that, she was convinced to be right. She needed to know what it meant, what Jake perceived their attraction to be. It took two to tango properly and just jumping into bed might well destroy the dance. Mostly, sex was never really love these days, not how it was presented in the media. That much Emma knew. It lacked what she was looking for: beauty in intimacy. Without it, she wasn't interested. But she carried an ache, an inescapable attraction, and that had to be love. It was rather unnerving. And Jake wasn't much for talking about his feelings, which didn't help at all.

Her mother had seen it right away, of course. Where did you find him? she whispered trying to hide her pleasure. In the pub, Emma said, tongue in cheek. She knew that mother wasn't that happy about her being a barmaid. Well, he seems to have got under your skin and I suggest you keep him there. Mother could be rather eloquent at times.

Jake had put his best foot forward with Emma's mother. She was home alone that day with dad on a ship and siblings busy elsewhere. He knows how to deal with people when he sets his mind to it, Emma thought. You just ask questions, Jake had once explained. That's what Joe had told her, if Emma remembered rightly. Perhaps he had not. Purposefully, she kept mostly silent making Jake hold the fort. Once mum got her talking hat on, and with Jake that one appeared almost instantly, there would be no lack of interaction anyway. Emma was fond of her mother, their differences long buried. It had been typical growing up stuff. Mum was a very embracing person.

Emma had taken Jake to Blythe to pick up her swag and borrow dad's car plus basic camping equipment. Dad wouldn't mind, he was that kind of father. In his car, a competent and comfortable Land Rover Discovery, they could safely enter the mountains. Emma had learned to drive vehicles well before sixteen. The age at which you could start learning for your official license. She had been bush with the family many a time. Dad liked getting away from everything into the rough stuff, including mountain climbs in the car. When she was a teenager, he let Emma behind the steering wheel occasionally. Some of these mountains she would now revisit. It was unlikely to include real climbing though. At least, she didn't think so.

At Orroroo they stretched their legs, bought a coffee, and sat down at a table with benches on the median strip. It was a neat, well-kept town with the council building in particular meticulously maintained. Like all major country towns it dated back into the later eighteen hundreds. Orroroo was on the road from Perth, many days driving to the west, to Sydney, two days minimum to the east. Cars with caravans were constantly travelling through. It was also the last real town when coming from the south heading north into the mountains of the Flinders Ranges. And perhaps beyond into real desert country. Emma liked Orroroo. She had years ago joined a girlfriend here for a rodeo. The friend competed in barrel racing, was mad about horses. It had been fun, with the country boys healthy and lusty. Always they were trying to score with the girls. The better riders and locally known Aussie Rules footballers were the most popular. Often their girlfriends came along keeping a close eye. With the police checking on alcohol levels everywhere few people would drive home at closing. Definitely not the younger ones. It made for a rowdy night. That had been when she still lived on their farm of course. One day she might be back to paint this pleasant streetscape, Emma mused, giving the scene another eye over.

'You think we'll find him?' Jake asked. He was looking at her closely. The country air had put a glow on Emma's face. She seemed more relaxed. At Blythe she had dug up her well-worn Akubra hat and thick-soled ankle height leather lace-up boots. She was wearing a loose rugged cotton shirt over a T-shirt and blue jeans. It left little doubt as to where she belonged, Jake thought.

Sitting here with Emma, on this pretty street well away from Adelaide, was great. They had not spent as much time together as both would have wished. With her always being busy and him holding a casual job as an orderly in a hospital with unpredictable shifts. He had taken the job to be amongst people for a while. Be at the coalface, to learn about life.

'Not sure whether we'll find him,' Emma admitted. 'We'll have a go.'

'Why do you feel he needs finding?'

When she had called suggesting the search, Jake did not ask many questions. Let's not be difficult when a good thing was staring you in the face. Off into the outback with Emma, could it get any better? He had told the hospital, he would be out of town for at least a week. As a casual worker that was not a problem.

Why indeed did she feel JH needed finding? Emma was unsure about her true motivation. Not that it really mattered. At first, she became convinced of the need for a search. It had been a spontaneous reaction. Those always came to bite you when rational thinking cut in. Rationality had its place, but could become a real killer of *joie de vivre*. Not in her life, Emma had once decided. Not if she could half help it. Perhaps the idea of spending quality time with Jake in the semi-wild was the real driver of her intentions. It was about time for them to live up close for a while. Finding out what that would be like. Either way, it would do – as a reason for going bush.

'Perhaps he doesn't need finding,' Emma conceded and smiled mischievously. 'Would you like to turn back?'

Jake grinned in response. 'He's a proper nomad you know. And there is not much phone connectivity in the mountains. But, I agree, we should have heard from him by now. Are we looking in the right direction though?'

'Definitely.' Emma was convinced of that.

Reluctantly, she had taken the liberty of entering JH's room looking for clues regarding his holiday. She found a discarded brochure of Arkaroola far up north in the Flinders near the end of the range. It confirmed what she was expecting.

JH had arrived at their doorstep with one large travel bag. The one he had taken to their houseboat weekend. From where he had travelled on for his holidays. He possessed little and preferred it that way. His clothes came from op-shops, though that never showed. Books he read came from the library or were downloaded on his notebook. The only book he carried with him was his dark-red leather-covered bible. Emma had found his room deserted of personal stuff, not because he would have left for good, but for the fact that taking along all he owned was necessary. That approach to life seemed a principle with JH. Not that he had ever said so. Emma just knew it to be typical of the man.

The first time she had noticed him reading his bible in the annex it surprised her. JH seemed not to fit the bill. That was silly, for Emma herself felt that she didn't really fit the bill either where it concerned her faith. On that point she was quite likely fooling herself. I didn't know you're a Christian, she had said. JH had responded that indeed he was. But he would use a different term. He was a Friend of Jesus. So, you're a Quaker, Emma wondered, from the Society of Friends? She knew of them from her readings in spirituality. JH appreciated the reference, but denied being a Quaker. Just an evolved Catholic, not associated with anyone, had been his reply. The term Christian carries too many negative connotations these days. It blurs the real intentions of Christ. He had smiled observing Emma's reaction to that idea. She just nodded her head, not taking the comment further, not then.

JH had kind eyes with a distinct sadness behind them. Later on, she learned why and was able to begin understanding it. She appreciated JH. Departing without prior notice about its finality, if indeed that was so, was completely out of character. Surely, something must have happened.

'We better get going,' she told Jake. 'You can drive, if you like.'

5

AT EMMA'S, ONE DAY, JH had asked Jake a question. Would he mind taking him to an Australian Rules football game? Having an interest in culture JH figured that this ball game was important to Adelaide. With the season about to begin, it was the talk of the town.

Jake no longer played Aussie Rules. He had at school but preferred cricket. Still, he readily accepted the idea. Adelaide supported two major teams. The first games of the year always found a keen interest. Jake didn't follow it much. However, a good scrap of footy would be fun. I will get us tickets, he told JH, for Sunday afternoon.

The Adelaide Oval offered a good sport experience. Recently modernised, it counted amongst the best venues in Australia. Though a large oval spectators remained in close proximity to the action. Sound reverberated around the stands and the noise level, once the crowd got excited, was impressive. At fever pitch you could hardly hear yourself speak. That Sunday, Jake had used the quieter moments to explain the game. They were seated on the western side in the shade. The roofs of the stands around the ground gave the idea of free floating parachutes, their white surface brightly reflecting the sun. The architecture of the stadium was striking.

JH seemed to enjoy all the commotion. He asked if they played with a rugby ball. Not quite, Jake told him, but the ball is similar. He explained the scoring system with the two high goal post and two shorter ones on either side at each end of the field. The ball kicked through the high posts gained six points unless touched by the opposition beforehand. That made it one point. Between a high and low post only one point was scored. The players, eighteen per team, were not allowed to throw the ball. Any other movement was fine. If the ball after being kicked was caught without anyone or the ground touching it, a player gained a "mark". Such a catch could make for a spectacular leap. You were allowed to play on from a mark with a free kick. Or a handball, a thump with a fisted hand against the ball that was held in the other. The speed and accuracy in which players were able to execute that motion was amazing. As was the distance over which it could make a ball fly. When tackled you had to dispatch the ball immediately.

The game was played over four quarters of twenty minutes real time. A clock kept count. Like gridiron. Jake figured that JH was familiar with the American game. A nod of his head confirmed it. Aussie Rules players are very fit, Jake explained, trained for speed and distance running. They had great mobility and were able to absorb serious clashes without body protection. Just like rugby. Jake left the finer points unexplained. Such as rules that minimized injury. It would become overly complicated. A game with its three rest breaks would last for well over two hours and remained fast throughout.

JH became taken up in the spectacle with a big smile. Obviously, sport was attractive to him. The local team won and the crowd exited the arena in high spirits. The game finished early in the evening which enticed folk to remain in the city for a drink and a bite to eat. Emma would be very busy in the pub tonight, Jake reflected. They were walking towards the CBD over a foot bridge that spanned the River Torrens. With JH, and a stream of others, they passed the Casino and

Adelaide Railway Station. How about a meal somewhere, my shout? JH suggested. He seemed relaxed and happy. Jake gladly agreed and decided to stay away from the Eastern part of town where Emma worked. Let's go to Gouger Street, he suggested, stretch our legs. The walk was not that far through the west side of the CBD.

They took a table in a Thai restaurant for a hot curry and a cool beer. Jake asked JH about his thoughts on Aussie Rules and the Oval.

Leaning back in his chair, JH said, 'Great place, great fun. But just a spectator.'

'You mean, emotional participation was low.'

'Yes. I could identify with it as sport, mostly.'

JH liked it, that Jake had grasped the point.

'Only belonging to the game will make an actual supporter,' Jake agreed.

It was an informed comment. 'What kind of stuff interests you, Jake?' JH wondered. 'I mean, your way of talking is rather astute.'

Jake looked at the man sitting across the table with his black hair, intelligent eyes and easy demeanour. He was good company and seemed interested. Jake sensed him to be well educated in spite of his unexceptional deportment. Fleetingly, he remembered his first date with Emma. That wonderful evening near the sea front. She had asked the same question. 'Philosophy,' he answered.

'Ah! In search of being.' JH nodded his head in appreciation. 'One of my interests.'

Jake's mention of philosophy came as no surprise, it seemed. Perhaps Emma had let the cat out of the bag. Jake drank some beer and gave the restaurant a look over. Busy, lots of people, all with a focus on their own affairs.

'Any particular kind of philosophy,' JH asked.

'Of the relational.'

That raised JH's eyebrows. 'Rather insightful,' he offered. 'It's the key to everything, in my view. How did you get to that?'

Jake had not expected such affirmation. Usually the responses to his interest were kind of guarded. People felt out of their depth. Except for a few uni friends. Many of whom had left Adelaide now. And the philosophy group he was a member of.

'My dad was a theologian with specific ideas about relationality. He died in an accident.' Jake mentioned this tragedy to pre-empt questions.

JH accepted that information without response.

'You know much about theology?' Jake asked. He might as well find out.

'Enough,' JH answered. He didn't elaborate.

Their meals arrived and for a while it concentrated their attention. The pavements at Gouger Street were always busy. It was popular for eating out with many options. Jake lazily observed the scene between bites.

'What about your father's ideas,' JH asked after a while. 'Would you mind telling me?'

Jake began to explain how Liam had developed the idea that "God is love" into a system of understanding that placed the relational at the centre of the universe, literally. That love was essentially relational and so was sin. These opposing dynamics had inescapable influences. Liam found support for this idea in theology, philosophy, psychology and science. From a study of the Trinity, he derived three fundamental, positive relational principles. In creation, these are opposed by three negative ones due to the power of sin. It made for six relational dynamics that operate with every person. The question was, which would have the upper hand? If the positive, it brought wellbeing. The negative resulted in disintegration of the psyche. Personal choice played a significant role, but not exclusively so. Every person had a relational imprint from previous experiences, which also was a deciding factor. Liam had designed a model of Trinitarian relating with outcomes for each principle in seven steps. It aligned with common sense and was practical.

JH listened carefully without interrupting. Finally, he asked whether a copy of Liam's ideas would be available.[1] Jake was happy to oblige. The request seemed genuine enough. While talking away, he had ignored his meal and for a while concentrated on the tasty food. JH drifted off into thought.

'So, what is your approach with the relational?' JH asked after a while.

'Not theological, but existential. I am interested in the relational based on human experience.'

'Which then ideally finds resonance in theology?' JH was testing how much credence Jake was willing to give to theological insights.

'Yes. But theology is related to a system of beliefs. If the relational is really that fundamental in our existence, it must be possible explain it free of religious input.'

'Like Harry Harlow's work with rhesus monkeys,' JH suggested.

---

[1] The model and the universal importance of love are presented in the book about Jake's desert adventure – *The Primacy of Love*

'Yes.'

Jake hadn't expected JH to know about this. But it was a famous experiment. Using young monkeys Harlow had shown that little ones, when deprived of affection, would deteriorate and eventually die. Those receiving much affection thrived. It highlighted the importance of love. Harlow's paper, "The nature of love", showed how the relational quality of our lives matters greatly. Strong physical bonds in infancy were needed to shape healthy adult lives. Not just in infancy, Jake believed. Though it determined much. All through life, the relational affected wellbeing.

But enough about the relational. Jake switched the conversation. 'What's your special interest?'

It was a fair enough question, JH thought.

'The Gospel. It has lost traction in our world and needs refocusing.' It was not a new idea, far from. But JH had his own thoughts about it.

That comment surprised Jake. He knew JH to be a Christian, but not about his theological interest. 'For what reason?' he wondered. Then sought the attention of a waitress. 'Like another beer?'

'Sure.' JH liked this Australian. He had planned a meal after the football game to find out more about him. Learning about his father's ideas was a pleasant surprise. JH was looking forward to receiving a copy. Clearly, Jake was following his father's footsteps, but differently.

'Yes, what's the reason?' JH repeated the question. He would keep it short.

'The two issues that interest me are the affective side of the Gospel and sin, how it is understood.. Both need further attending too, I believe.'

Jake just listened.

'Theology and doctrine are prominent, but support structures of the real thing. Too easily they are seen as sufficient by themselves. The affective implications are considerable. I can't elaborate on that right now.'

'And what about sin?' Jake asked.

'Yes. There is the problem of sin,' JH continued. 'Holding Adam and Eve responsible is overly simplistic.'

'It's just a myth,' Jake said. At least that was what he believed.

'Whatever your view, the story has a lot of meaning. Many consider it the foremost explanation of why all of us are exposed to our world's destructive powers.'

'Sin existed way before Adam and Eve,' Jake said, remembering his father's ideas.'

'It did. But further thoughts on that will be helpful.'

'After two thousand years?' Jake was sceptical. But he always liked someone having new ideas. 'Perhaps, I'm dining with a heretic,' he suggested tongue in cheek.

'Perhaps.' JH smiled. 'They have burned perfectly righteous men at the stake. That's unlikely in my case.'

Jake was intrigued. 'What's your motivation?'

'It concerns me, that generally God is insufficiently understood. If you wonder how that might be possible, well, just consider church history. The ridiculous things done in the name of Christ are unbelievable. Our times have their own problems regarding the presentation of Good News.'

JH looked through the window out into the street, now getting dark. Jake decided to again change topics. He took a mouthful of beer.

'What brought you to Australia?' he asked.

JH considered this young philosopher. One day he would explain his interests further, if the occasion arose.

"I'm interested in people and culture. Finding out what the world is like away from South America. People and countries are fascinating, everywhere.'

'You've been around?' Jake wondered.

'A little. Australia is my second stopover.'

'Your English is very good,' Jake complimented him.

'I have lived in the States for a while.' JH didn't mention that it had been on a prominent scholarship.

He was good company, Jake concluded. He liked his type of person. Perhaps they would talk some more. Not today though. It was time to make for home.

6

THE CAR PULLED UP in front of the sign Beltana. It hang off a high pole that rested on two white posts, each of which had a wagon wheel standing up beside it. The old frontier town was now mostly deserted, but not quite. Some privately owned buildings could be inhabited. There were ruins scattered about, testimony that over a century ago this had been a thriving settlement housing some 500 people. Amongst the buildings in those early days was a courthouse, a number of pubs and dwellings necessary for a variety of trades to function. Beltana was a tourist attraction these days and surrounded by a sheep and cattle station. The old railway line had long been demolished and the new highway ran well west. The copper mine, the reason for the town's original existence, was declared uneconomical long ago. Afghan camel trains were a memory of the by-gone past. Still, Beltana had a claim to fame that was unlikely to be forgotten.

In 1911 the Presbyterian Church sent out its next missionary, Rev John Flynn. For little over a year, at the age of thirty, he looked after the spiritual care of Beltana and settlers living many miles away. Though his stay was brief, Flynn had become acutely aware of the scarcity of medical assistance. Much so in serious cases. Throughout outback Australia the same problem existed. From the humble beginnings of enlisting nurses with the task of helping people in remote regions either personally or by phone, Flynn established Australia's Flying Doctor services. It was to transport the seriously ill or hurt from far-away places to suitable care facilities by plane. The service remains active, and important, today.

Emma slid out of the cabin of the Land Rover holding her camera with a wide angle lens. Though not as dusty as might be expected in summer, the land looked sparse and barren. Saltbush, blue bush and acacias were the native vegetation. Along the creeks gum trees grew. It was country in which life-stock holdings would become profitable and ecologically responsible when animals grazed over vast areas. Even then, farming remained a dicey business, not always paying the bills. She looked towards the mountains on the horizon. They had followed the Flinders Ranges north over flat open land for many miles keeping the range at their right.

Jake stepped out from behind the steering wheel and pulled his shoulders back in a stretch, his lanky frame supple and solid with the wind blowing through his blond hair. Emma thought it a beautiful sight. A vibrant modern man, with some outback ruins not far behind him. Hope envisaged, and hope spent. An artist might paint this, Emma thought. Somehow express those two sides of hope. But it wouldn't be her. Not with Jake in the picture. She would be too emotionally distracted to do the task justice. That clear observant eye needed for good art, being detached from its object to a measure, surely would desert her. Emma looked away giving attention to her camera instead. When faced with interesting buildings she tended to take pictures. Historic bush structures not excluded.

She suggested they'd wander about separately. Jake could follow his own interests. Sure, he agreed, accepting that easily. The sky was clear, a slow wind blew, and light brightened the landscape with the diminished intensity usual for winter when the sun stood lower in the sky. Emma was feasting on the sense of space and an ancient environment – millions of years old, in fact. It stirred her soul. This must be Eros, she thought. JH once had briefly explained that idea to Ruth and herself. Art had got a mention. Trust JH to have something meaningful to say.

A definitive answer to the question, "what is art?", or "what is beauty?" for that matter, would never be given. That much she had learned at university. But JH had raised the issue of why it was meaningful to ask such questions in the first place. Why the human drive towards art and beauty? Or, more exactly, what was it that drew you towards these qualities, made you pursue them? It was the human capacity to become enchanted with Eros, he had explained. The first thoughts modern people had when Eros is mentioned usually concerned sex. However Eros, as merely the sexy side of love, simply didn't do the ancient idea justice. An idea that had originated from the Greek myths and the days of Socrates and Plato. Eros involved passion. It concerned a being stirred on towards understanding and achievement in all kinds of quests, including art - and relationships. Emma had found JH's explanation rather helpful. It had become a substantial discussion with Ruth and herself asking him questions. She had been able to make better sense of her feelings and experiences since. Being in love was both surprising and unnerving. And there were pitfalls.

Walking around the ruins and old buildings of Beltana, Jake followed Emma's progress over a distance. He couldn't keep his eyes off her. Perhaps it was the outback, which she seemed so attuned to. He was careful not to stare. If Emma noticed his attention, she gave no sign of it. Never looked at him. She was fully concentrated on her photography, finding the angles and shade patterns to make a good picture. Jake felt his groin stir. He made a concentrated effort in looking away. Emma deserved her space.

Leaving Orroroo, they had taken the RM Williams Drive toward Hawker, the road climbing steadily until they were well and truly in mountain country. As so often in inland Australia – the road was good with little traffic. Emma considered it one of her favourites. It was simultaneously gentle and rugged, she observed. A rather apt description, Jake thought. He enjoyed the driving, more so because the car was in cruise control.

At Hawker they had stopped for diesel and bought a meat pie at the service station. Their enquiry about a South American looking man with a scar on his left cheek travelling through lately found no affirmative answer. Serving so many travellers, for Hawker was the place to tank when heading north, or coming back from there, the attendant couldn't be sure. Let's check at the caravan park, Emma had suggested. No luck there either. With many places available to stay the night, if you were willing to travel long distances, it was unsurprising.

The most northerly destination they planned to visit was Arkaroola. JH would almost certainly have aimed for that wilderness sanctuary. From Hawker there were two routes available to Arkaroola. They had decided to follow the least cumbersome with a last stretch over maintained dirt roads. Beltana would be their overnight stopover.

'How are you, cobber?' Emma said with a smile, coming towards Jake walking uphill, her camera held loosely in one hand. Smitten, if she really wanted to know.

'Fine.'

'We'd better drive to the homestead, find a place to camp. It's not far.'

'Sure.' Jake pulled himself together. Already when still in Adelaide he had decided to keep his desires in check. Doing otherwise could be fatal. Care was of the order. Still, it was difficult to argue with your feelings; you simply needed to keep them controlled. He gave Emma a genuine smile and dug for the car keys in his pockets to hand them over. Emma shook her head. She would happily be a passenger for now.

Soon the station yard and the homestead came into view. Many stations up north accommodated travellers for welcome extra income. As always, the people out bush were friendly. If you didn't arrive with airs and graces. It was tough country out here conquered in no-nonsense ways. Emma felt right at home.

They were directed to a fine spot with a lovely view. Firewood was to be delivered and should only be used in the designated pit. The sky was clear. Soon a chill would settle over the land. It would be cold. Just what the doctor ordered, Emma thought. Nothing beats a wood fire to keep you warm. Also, she loved the crisp mornings that followed a frost. Whether it would actually freeze tonight, she didn't know. She would sleep under the branches of a lone she-oak nearby. Hear it whistling in the wind, soothing her to sleep. She felt happy.

Split blocks of sugar gum arrived and they got a fire going. It would be dark early. Cooking before it fell was best. Soon the sausages thrown into a long-handled skillet placed upon hot coals began to sizzle. Emma would add mini spuds from a tin later for browning. She placed an open tin of sweet corn into the smouldering ashes. It had been too long since she last prepared a meal on an open fire. Quietly she decided to camp outdoors more often.

Jake watched it all sitting leisurely in his folding chair. He could have cooked himself, being well able since that desert trip with Baz. He enjoyed seeing Emma so obviously in her element. It added to his desire for her.

'Why don't you open a bottle of red, Jake?' They had brought some decent wines along.

Jake selected a Shiraz from the Barossa and searched for wine glasses. Wine, out bush, should not be drunk out of plastic. A thin edged glass made it taste so much better, somehow. Hopefully, the glasses would last the distance.

They ate in silence and ended up staring into the fire. Each with their own thoughts. Jake remembered his last night with Baz at the creek near the Farina ruins about sixty miles further north. Baz had talked about love's day in court that evening. His final explanation of Liam's thoughts. Jake had just listened, not asking questions. They had sat around a fire just like today. Sitting close to Emma, the memories of his father brought on a pang of sorrow. "If only?" Dad, in his all-embracing manner, would have been so happy meeting her. But there was no if. Never would be.

Emma observed Jake with tumbling emotions. Had she been selfish with that spontaneous suggestion of joining her camping? That wasn't so. Sure, being in close proximity in the middle of nowhere would present problems. But their relationship over the past months warranted it. She could have never gone without him. Jake would have been horrified had she not wanted him along. His face looked troubled, Emma thought. Perhaps her presence was to blame. It would be best to bell the cat. Emma believed in being up front in situations that could become difficult. She searched for the right words.

'You're looking sad, Jake. Is it because of me?'

Jake startled out of his reverie. Took a moment to grasp the context of Emma's question. He shook his head, as if waking up. It became clear to Emma that she had got it wrong. 'Sorry, Emma. My thoughts took me away.' He refrained from explaining.

'But, if you feel for me, what I feel for you, being together could become problematic,' Emma pressed on. She didn't like to, but it would be better that way.

Jake was taken aback. This conversation took an unexpected turn. He looked at Emma carefully and found her serious and considerate. A faint smile was playing on her face. He was left for words and just nodded.

Emma felt real pity for him. It came unsolicited. She sensed that Jake was nursing a serious grief. Probably the loss of his father. Not that he was about to tell her. Such a closed-up guy. That would change, if she had any say in it. Her stomach churned in empathy. Almost she got up to grab him hard, but knew not to. With effort and some deep breathing she subdued her emotions. Better get it out and over with.

'We will be sleeping close to each other for a number of nights,' Emma continued. She looked away from Jake, into the fire. 'One day I'll be ready for sex, but not yet. I will know the moment.'

That was up-front talking. The flames played havoc with the dry wood. Jake hid his surprise, still making no comment. Emma felt agitated. This was not an easy for her and some response would be appreciated.

'Then, you can fuck me,' she said. She found an edge in the coarse language. It showed the passion she felt. Sex tapped into deep waters.

Jake looked at her face in the darkness. Her troubled look onto which the fire projected its shadows. 'Sorry, Emma,' he said softly, 'I understand.'

'Thanks,' she mumbled.

Jake said what he felt. 'I have no wish to just fuck you, Emma. Not unless I can make love to you.'

The words hung in the air as if reluctant to dissipate. Emma understood it well. The intimacy of genuine love making required considerable give and take – could be intense. It was deeply personal and overwhelming. Like a pressure valve being released. She sensed that intuitively and could feel pressure moving within her. They were not ready for it - certainly she wasn't.

'Thanks, Jake,' she said once more. Her eyes were moistening up. This postponing might become harder than imagined. Neither spoke for a while.

Then Jake asked, 'Do you remember that Idea I told you about, the philosophy of the relational and living it out?'

Emma did. Their first date, and his presentation at the philosophy group a few weeks ago.

'I agree with you. In the relational, second best, is not great.' It was a principle he had decided to live by. Life worked best that way.

'Ever the philosopher, hey,' Emma smiled faintly. 'Don't change, Jake.'

Not likely, he thought. And felt closer to her now than ever before. He said the words he found so difficult to speak out, because of his reserved nature. 'I love you, Emma.'

She sat bent over. Her head down and arms folded across her chest. Emotions were racing. A beanie pulled tight over her ears against the cold. She just nodded.

Jake stared into the fire. It was dimming and needed wood. He was glad to have said the words and never would find them easy.

'I'm off finding my swag,' Emma said hoarsely. 'I'll kiss you in the morning.' It was the only way, she could handle the situation.

'Sure thing.'

Jake felt melancholy setting upon him. He would stay in the wide open night, under a starry sky, a little longer. His thoughts returned to his dad. He couldn't help it. His love for Emma seemed to make his loss more acute. The outback did that to you. Help you confront your deeper soul. Perhaps because out in the open your defences were breached. In a positive way if you allowed it to happen. Jake just sat looking into the dying embers. This melancholy was a gently one. It felt like a kind of healing. The movements of love were surprising.

.

7

AT COPLEY they took a right turn off the bitumen onto dirt. Arkaroola was a little over two hours away. Emma was driving and felt happy. They had slept in till daylight proper with the sun still obscured by the mountains. The journey ahead was not a long. She had embraced Jake as promised. He had shown some welcome male aggression, just enough. Perfect, Emma thought. After all, she had grown up amongst the "cowboys." She was in love, head over heels now. No sex though, she had decided. Much easier. Most likely their camping would be for a few days only anyway. Keeping Eros in check might be difficult though. JH had explained it well. Would they actually find him? Emma had her doubts.

'What do you know about Eros, Jake?' she asked spur of the moment. It was kind of relevant. She kept a sharp eye on the road. Holes and rock were the main car wreckers. It was obvious though that the surface had not long ago been graded At least, the section they were currently travelling through. It being popular with tourist road was well maintained.

Jake felt a kind of mental jolt. From easy reflection into a necessary focus. Trust Emma to ask a question like that. In the middle of nowhere.

'Why now?'

'Go figure. Surely you know why?' Emma grinned, briefly looking sideways at him. That Jake could make the connection between her question and their circumstances was a given.

'Eros is the god of love in Greek mythology,' he offered.

'Wow,' Emma goaded him, tongue in cheek.

'It is also a favourite topic of JH, it seems,' he added. He rather would not take up the subject right now. Emma looked happy. It would have brought on the question.

Eros personified, that was her state of being that morning, Emma thought. Love and passion – a forceful surge of life. Why not talk about it? She should allow Jake space though. 'Don't worry. It can wait.'

'Sure.' Jake dropped back into a comfortable mood with ease, satisfied with saying little.

Emma didn't mind. Her thoughts drifted back to that one evening.

Occasionally, Ruth and she made a concerted effort towards time together as friends. They would prepare a nice dinner with a few good wines and enjoyed expensive chocolates. They kept their conversations meaningful, avoiding any mention of work. Ruth, as a social worker, would have plenty of stories to tell. Emma never liked talking about her job anyway. She preferred art and the intuitive side of life. One day, well into one of their chinwags, the front door clicked open. JH passed by heading for his room. He said a quick hello.

'Just the man we're looking for,' Ruth exclaimed.

That could be true enough, Emma thought.

'We're discussing how life seems to be scripted with everything pre-packaged for our consumption in the way the media, commercial gurus and politicians decide. The only unpredictable thing left is sport, and even that can be rigged.'

JH stood listening attentively.

Ruth continued. 'Somehow everyday life has been bedded down. For all the benefits of modern technology, it seems kind of bland.' That seemed a decent summary.

Emma watched JH with interest. His intelligent eyes sparkled and a faint smile played on his face. One of understanding rather than mockery.

'Come join us, JH,' she suggested. 'We have some Argentinean red left in the bottle.'

He sat down not saying a word. Emma got up to find a glass. Ruth looked at her South American housemate with interest. He was able to comment on all sorts of issues rather well, she knew. If he would ever ask her out, which was unlikely, she would agree immediately.

'Have a chocolate,' she offered handing him the box. He selected one and waited for Emma to pour out a red.

'The suppression of Eros,' JH said.

Both Ruth and Emma just stared at him.

'Do you mean sex?' Ruth ventured carefully. It didn't make sense.

JH smiled. 'That's the popular meaning given to Eros today, but originally it involved so much more.'

He explained that in early Greek mythology Eros was the god of love. He created the world and brought life, joy and motion to what had been silent, bare and motionless. Over time this mythology developed into Eros being the little son of the gods Aphrodite and

Ares. Eros remained rather cupid-like, lacking in growth and not at all assertive. An oracle declared that, "Love cannot grow without passion."

'When passion is on a slow burner, the true potential of humanity will suffer,' JH said. 'People these days are living in a manner that is conditioned towards keeping everything on an even keel. Don't raising too many issues. Look after yourself and enjoy it when you can. It's not bad, if you like it that way. But is that a life well lived? It lacks the pleasures and frustrations of Eros.'

'Go on,' Emma said, when JH halted.

'Yes,' Ruth agreed. This was good stuff.

'Eros concerns the daimonic.' JH spelled the word out. 'Not to be confused with the demonic, which is destructive and an expression of it. The daimonic is a force more elementary than good and evil. Our primary drive towards self-assertion. You might call it the most fundamental dynamic within the human spirit.'

The ideas of Jake's father were somewhat similar. Love and sin that pre-existed good and evil, which were derivatives of it. JH saw no need to mention that.

'The daimonic is able to express good as well as evil. The extent of it much depends on the human psyche.'

'So it can be both a blessing and a curse,' Emma suggested.

'Yes. Most of us live in ignorance of it though. It limits our authenticity.'

'Why?' Ruth asked.

'We fail to acknowledge the importance of living passionately for a truly meaningful life. By passion, I don't mean some kind of hot-and-bothered engagement with a given issue. But that fervent interest, that enthusiasm for what stirs you deeply. Having something to commit to that keeps your juices going. Without it we will not reach self-expression at significant levels. One uniquely ours.'

JH continued.

'Modern life manipulates us into a false sense of individuality. The idea that in driving the right car, buying the good house and having our expensive holidays we achieve intrinsic worth as a person.'

That was true enough, Emma thought.

'Social commentators, like Allan Bloom, lament the loss of true Eros in society. Everything becomes analysed and deconstructed. Science tells us we are nothing special really. Pawns in a grey mass of humanity. The measure of the person has become determined by fame, money or cleverness. Down the pecking order, you are really just an evolved animal, driven to copulate, to spend and to die into oblivion. Under the deceptive banner of equality everyone becomes nobody. Even if you sense you are actually someone. Technology goads us into the idea of progress, but feelings of alienation are increasing.'

'And that's why we feel uneasy,' Ruth offered. 'What Emma and I were discussing.'

'Yes. Obviously, you are sensitive to something lacking. The daimonic is nudging you. You, being well-adapted, should be able to find an answer that is positive. But if you felt disenfranchised by society and feel unable to achieve the identity you sense to deserve, that nudging could turn to the negative. Translate into fascination with acts of violence, or to actually becoming violent.'

'The demonic,' Emma suggested.

'In serious manifestations - yes.'

JH continued.

'Disenfranchisement is relational. You could say that almost everyone these days has become disempowered from Eros. Its true meaning. The notion of love in our society has turned bland. It has lost depth and integrity. It's mostly associated with superficial sex. Where is the true lover? The giver genuinely concerned with the other, who yet takes with passion? I'm not sure people would know how to aspire to that. It requires a sense of humility and of care. That is seldom discussed these days. You have to tap deeply into your psyche. It means paying a price, being unselfish and giving. But it enables you to receive, to take and become intimately unified with another person.'

'You have been there, have you?' Emma wondered. The question came spontaneously. She remembered his sad eyes. 'Has Eros lamed you, like Jacob perhaps?' Where on earth did that come from?

JH flinched and momentarily his relaxed demeanour changed. Emma noticed a glimpse of a deep hurt in the man. She should have figured.

'Sorry,' she offered. 'I didn't mean to be personal.'

'It's fine. That was insightful,' JH responded. An image of Eva drifted across his mind. Her beauty and lust for life. He gave it some thought and decided to tell his story. It might help in explaining the pitfalls of Eros.

'I met a girl one day who completely took my heart. I had no idea that such an experience was possible. You cannot prepare for that. Love is blind, they say, and so was mine.'

Emma was thinking of Jake. She didn't feel as if she was racing up a blind alley though.

'We loved and made love passionately. We got married impulsively. Eva was so full-on in all she did. A wonderful person. Unfortunately, her sexual desire was burning at a level way beyond mine. All was fine at first, but slowly we became less intimate and more daring.'

JH sipped the last of his wine. Emma replenished his glass. Ruth had nestled completely into the back of her chair for all the comfort she could get.

'Eva was an adventurer in many ways. One was body exploration. I set some boundaries. They were tolerated with a gentle smile of disappointment. What used to be a meeting of two hearts became a search for satisfaction. Not often would we get beyond that now.'

JH looked at his companions. They were sitting motionlessly. Perhaps he should have refrained from telling his story.

'We became emotionally separated. Eva began to tire of me and eventually found someone else. She was never nasty though, always fun, and full of energy. Passion was her signature mood. That's Eros for you, the daimonic. I still love her.'

Emma just sat there. Ruth seemed miles away.

'I was aiming high,' JH concluded his story. 'I came up short. That's okay.'

He well knew that aiming for love over and against

erotism was not a shortcoming. It didn't much help in diminishing his loss though. Sensing the silence that had come over his companions JH decided to break it by mentioning a more common manifestation of Eros.

'One of the more usual expressions of Eros is our fascination with sport. Identifying with a given team and thus feeling lifted out of the drudgery of daily life. The commitment, the love of the club's history, the highs and the lows, all may be seen as part of Eros. Eros pulls you towards it, you could say, fires up your desires. Emotions run deeply. It's why sport is so attractive, I believe.'

'But is may turn nasty, like soccer hooliganism. Some sports, by their very nature, tap into the daimonic in a negative way. Boxing and international wrestling are an example. The shouts of the audience speak volumes. The popularity of violence in films is another. Not to speak of religious wars that are raging around the globe. When people feel disempowered and incapable of Eros, they seem to compensate towards the negative.'

It was not something she would have thought of, Emma concluded. But it made sense.

'And what if sport doesn't appeal to you?' Ruth had broken out of her reverie.

JH gave her a smile. 'There are better ways. In

sport you are connecting with an event beyond yourself over which you have little control. But you identify with it. The dynamics of the team captivate you. Whole societies can be taken up with that, feel its effects. Like winning a world cup. But Eros is most personal when it arises solely from within your own self. The urge you feel rising up, that desire that simply seems to be you. That which you love and has your passion. You answer it with purpose and develop as a person accordingly. It will make demands. But you know its value and by committing to it rise above the mundane in life.'

'Like my fascination with art,' Emma suggested.

'Yes. Or you may work at being a fine person to be with. You may collect stamps, for that matter. Write music or books and study nature. Anything positive and meaningful that stirs your heart. It attracts you and brings significance into your life. You will then know personally that life need not be mundane per se.'

JH looked at them. He had said enough. 'One day we may talk some more perhaps,' he suggested. 'But you were right, Emma. There is a price to be paid. Jacob has a lame leg. After all, Eros is the god of love. And love costs.'

Emma was slowing down to traverse a creek bed, nothing complicated. That had been quite a night. Both Ruth and she had learned a lot. She remembered finding her bed a little punch drunk. Thoughts about Jake had tumbled through her head. Their relationship and her art was Eros to her. JH had brought matters nicely into perspective.

Not far to Arkaroola now. They were on the final stretch.

8

THE PHILOSOPHY GROUP was seated in easy chairs. Among them Emma and JH who had been invited as guests. Jake was presenting a paper. The group counted about half a dozen members of varied backgrounds. The atmosphere, as usual, was relaxed. There would be no sharpening of intellectual swords this evening. Showing interest in the ideas a member had on offer was the main objective. With comments and question when considered helpful. The group did not lean towards particular points of view. If your concepts were reasonable, in the true sense of the word, you were welcome to them. All were familiar with the thoughts of Jake's father. Jake had once mentioned what made him have such an interest in the relational. It led to distributing an outline of Liam's ideas. A few in the group were Christians. The others had keen interest in creative thinking about human existence, whatever the source. After some small-talk everyone settled to hear what Jake had come to share. Emma felt a little nervous. Would she be out of her depth?

'Please take a copy of some notes,' Jake suggested. 'They are skimpy, but may help in guiding your thoughts. I will put some flesh on the bones.'

He remained seated, like the others, but on the edge of his chair.

'You would have read the theological ideas of my father. His model of relational interaction that functions within every individual person, between people and from people towards their environment. The question is: can you come to these insights without theological input, solely based on human experience. The information can then not be written off as just the reflections of a man determined by his religious views. I have no qualms in declaring a personal belief in God. But do not intend to let that influence my question, which will be answered philosophical. I will share some initial thoughts today.'

Emma listened intently. She would ask Jake for a copy of that model by his father.

'Hollywood tends to pre-show a movie before its

release. It is interested in audience feedback. With one now well-known film the viewers responded negatively. The ending grated. It lacked redeeming factors. Didn't bring happiness. The relational was central to the script and the viewers disliked the final scenes. It reflected real life well enough. But hey - this was the movies. The actors were recalled for a reshoot. The film sold well, now with a good ending.

'I would like to consider the implications of the word "good", as in a good ending. As you know, thousands of years ago Plato suggested the importance of "the Good". An idea he must have learned from Socrates. The best life would aim for that which was good. For Aristotle "the Good" came to mean what is best called happiness. Then, as now, people desired the furtherance of good. For it brought wellbeing. Life experience supported that idea. That good and happiness are important has a long history.

'These qualities affect us. Their dynamic is relational. Something within me becomes influenced. You could say that about conscious processes in general. My thoughts influence me. So do my emotions and intuition. Even my subconscious works its effects, psychology tells me. In essence, I am a relation. And I relate. To myself, other, and the world. A comprehensive understanding of the relational is thus important. That includes a philosophical perspective.'

Jake glanced at his notes.

'What is the best relational experience I might ever have? Friendship would be high on the list. But even better, that which always makes books and films popular. It is love. That greatest good and value everyone yearns for. A simple statement like, "love one another", needs no divine decree to confirm its validity. It rings true to what is best in life. No education is required to figure it out. We know it to be true. That love brings well-being and is good for everyone. Harry Harlow's experiments with monkeys proved it and is unlikely to have surprised many. The point here to remember is that we *know* it to be true. It is *truth*, and we just know that! Whether we live it out is secondary.

'Love is the ultimate positive relational dynamic in our lives. My father would have added, in the universe and beyond. Love is a truth, and of the highest value. When considering the relational philosophically - what allows for the good life - this highest value will be my starting point. How then may the ultimate good, its nature and influences everywhere, be explained?'

Jake gathered his thoughts.

'But much of life is far from good,' the only lady in

the group, apart from Emma, remarked. 'Surely you need to accommodate for that.'

'Yes, thanks,' Jake responded. 'That's right. Today, I will focus on the up-side. Our reality is ontologically a positive/negative one. The truth of love is opposed by what we know as sin. Sin is by nature as relational as love, but towards the destructive. It will feature in my thinking and intentions as the opposite of love. When love and its influences are subdued.'

He continued.

'You can engage with philosophy as a discipline in many ways. I will be guided by French philosopher Alain Badiou in my approach. He has been called a thinker of the Idea, written with a capital I. In explaining this let me quote from his book *Philosophy and the Event*.

> There is grandeur and dignity to the Idea. Elevating oneself to Ideas is a mode of being and living that human beings can make their own, and thereby realise that life is worthwhile being experienced to the full, and that a part - the most precious part - of themselves depends on this.[2]

'The Idea represents truth, and must be accessible

---

[2] Badiou, A 2013, *Philosophy and the Event*, Polity Press, UK p.147

to every person, regardless of his or her station in life. Badiou insists that in its presentation of an Idea, philosophy should be sure that it can be personally embraced and lived out by everyone, anywhere. The Idea must be able to inspire a movement or conviction from *within* the person.

'I really like that,' Jake said. 'Obviously love, fits the requirements of such an Idea perfectly. It is truth and intrinsically available to every person.'

Emma became captivated. Philosophy was more interesting than she had expected. I'm in love and living it out, she thought.

'In the history of philosophy, thinkers who take love as their starting point are hard to find. Hegel appears to have considered it in his earlier thoughts, but never persisted. To him love takes us beyond the natural world. For my purposes, I hold that love *is* our natural world. Its influences are fundamental and all important. Without the realities of love, however indistinguishable at times, we would all shrivel up. The power of love in our lives is real and true. And, as may be expected, philosophy is not in ignorance of love.

'But philosophy's dealing with the word mostly involves an observation of its properties in relation to other ideas. Usage of the word is descriptive at best and assumed as simply understood in most cases. Love is not analysed for its own sake, its meaning probed. That is considered better suited to literature. But the insights gained from literature are generally too limiting. They don't justify using love as an Idea. The Idea must be non-exclusive and readily available to everyone. Philosopher Hannah Arendt upholds the common literary view when beginning one of her sentences with: "For love, although it is one of the rarest occurrences in human lives ....." Most people would ascribe to this. What love really is about – a deeply falling in love. It is elusive. It doesn't happen to every person. While the love I am suggesting is available to all. So, what then, is love?

'My father considered the practical side of love best described as care. He supplemented that with the qualities of responsibility and integrity. They, in essence, are part of good caring. Everyone can care, if they so decide. If that reminds us of Heidegger and his philosophy of "I care", that needs qualification. Heidegger's notion is ego-centric. Martin Buber concluded that with regard to other people Heidegger proposed carefulness rather than care.

Buber is, of course, known for the I-Thou concept. It involves the spiritual side of being human. In the sense that everyone is a spiritual person irrespective of belief. I believe that genuine relating is an activity that issues from the human spirit. From a level in our being that precedes the cognitive and emotional. Buber has much to say about the relational that is worthwhile. However, for Love as an Idea, a less esoteric exposition is needed.

Jake took a break. 'Any questions?' he asked.

'You are suggesting that love and the good are synonymous. Right?' A young nerdish looking man asked.

'The good is an expression of love. I consider it to be a derivative. Good as an act is the non-emotional experience of love,' Jake explained.

'Like, love you neighbour as yourself,' the young man remarked. 'You are not expected to be in love with that person.' He nodded his head thoughtfully.

'Yes, in that statement the word love is used in reference to doing good. It makes the point nicely.'

'Just a clarification,' an older man said. 'So love is the ultimate in the relational. Something to aim for. But the relational itself is broader than love?'

'Yes. As said earlier, the relational also concerns the negative, the dynamics of sin.'

'Okay. Is then all relational expression that is not

related to sin one of love? Or vice versa.'

Jake smiled. He well understood the intent of Ian's question. 'Or, is there a neutral area, neither love nor sin, you are asking?'

'If you wish.'

'I don't know,' Jake admitted. 'It depends how you conceptually deal with it. Checking in with our feelings, there probably is a neutral zone. Information comes our way that is neither here nor there. The intake of any information is always relational for it affects me. Even though this affect may translate into a non-event within my psyche, it still remains a non-event relationally. There is never a vacuum in the relational. I would like to say that as a non-event is not affecting me negatively, it may be classified as good. But I would have no problem with a neutral zone. Which is not as large as generally thought. People are sensitive beings. They tend to nuance their feelings quickly.'

No further questions were raised. Emma noticed that JH had an appreciative look on his face. He was enjoying himself.

'Okay.' Jake collected his thoughts. 'Let's now continue with a comments about psychology. Because of the nature of the discipline it may be expected that the concept of love is there better dealt with. It is true.

Rollo May's *Love and Will* and *The Art of Loving* by psychiatrist Erich Fromm, which became a best seller, are an example. Not forgetting to mention *The Road Less Travelled* by M. Scott Peck. He admits that to his knowledge no-one has given a satisfactory definition of love. For his purposes he defines love as our self extending itself towards spiritual growth. Scott Peck holds that love is not a feeling, but a constructive action. We touched on that with the "love your neighbour" concept. But no-one, who has ever been exposed to love emotionally, would argue against it being a feeling as well. We may readily conclude then that love can be a feeling or an action, or both. It can even simply be a positive intent.

'Psychology has analysed the human condition extensively. Techniques about coping with life are plentiful. The popularity of self-help books never seems to wane. The desire of success and happiness is at the forefront of human intention. However, what is good and worthwhile is not as easily attained as many writers make believe. Happiness, for instance, is best achieved by the building of character, which always is a slow process, according to psychologist Martin Seligman. Aristotle, in antiquity, already came to a similar conclusion. That virtues are the way to happiness. The title of Seligman's book is a real publisher's concoction: *Authentic Happiness: Using the New Positive Psychology to Realise Your Potential for Lasting Fulfilment.* Character building is classified as a New Positive Psychology. But at least, Seligman is honest about the difficulties. He offers the benefits as possible. Bertrand Russell also recognised the hard work involved with happiness and gave his book the title: *The Conquest of Happiness.* His suggests to become less preoccupied with the self and more with others.'

It was brief, these comments about the soul.

'I mentioned Alain Badiou and his approach to philosophy. It involves the Idea. The Idea must be truth. It must be accessible to everyone. The Idea should be lived out personally by the philosopher. The Idea must also allow any person to develop authentically, to find a personal identity that is not cowed by society. I proposed that Love is such an Idea.

'Alain Badiou has written a book *In Praise of Love*, one of few philosophers to do so. His view is that Christianity has understood the importance of love accurately. But it became elevated it into transcendence to the level of otherworldliness. While modern society is now timid on the possibilities of love. Bringing love down to earth at the one hand, and elevating it at the other, is what interests me. To show it as possible, practical and way out there when it presents that way. Love as experience.'

Jake gathered his thoughts. So far, so good.

'In closing, I will briefly consider the world we live in. Philosophy is concerned with the diagnostic of our times. That's a massive undertaking. In the West we are rich as never before. But the world is in flux as never before. People feel swamped and overloaded. Thus held at bay from their true selves, if that fact even occurs to them. Is there, in all this busyness, a way to anchor your life? A fix that will not drift in the sands? A personal conviction that will stand the testing of our times. One that can be lived by. A foundation that allows you to rise up above the fog of confusion that covers so much. In fact, you need an Idea. An Idea that offers potential. It must be formulated in a way that convinces you of its value. You must feel enabled to make it *your* anchor stuck into *your* foundation. The Idea must be practical.'

Jake stopped briefly before making a final comment. Time was running out.

'In modern society, however you like to interpret it, people want interconnectedness. The younger ones in particular. My generation senses that selfishness should be transcended. It aspires to an identity that outlasts indiscriminate change. An authenticity that helps you cope with life. It needs a psychologically deep reaching worldview. It needs an Idea. I propose Love, with all its influences and implications, to be such an Idea. It's non-cultural and never loses its value. It is relational to the core and central to being human. It can be philosophy.'

Jake shifted into the back of his easy chair looking slightly drained.

Emma could hardly describe her feelings. It was a mixture of admiration, empathy and sheer joy. How had she ever come across this guy? Life is good to me, she concluded. How wonderful the good can be.

JH made an observation. 'One of your points is that the functionality of love within our psyche has never been presented so that the ordinary person can easily grasp the idea. How you can *do* love, you might call it. I assume that to be part of your research.'

'Yes,' Jake agreed. JH nicely made an important point. 'My father had significant insights on that, which I will take as a guide.'

'That's fair enough,' the chairman said. 'Thank you Jake. That was thought provoking. Time is moving on. If anyone has questions, perhaps those can be put to Jake over a cuppa. Ian will present at our next meeting. We're looking forward to that.'

JH mingled easily amongst the group. Emma felt less confident. She soon discovered that those aspiring to philosophy can be nice people.

9

ARKAROOLA WOULD SOON come within sight. Emma remembered it from years ago. Before it became a well-known tourist destination. Often she had wished to visit the place again, but that never happened. Much had changed and been improved since her previous stay. The road from Copley for instance now featured an all-weather dirt surface. No slipping and sliding in the mud when bad weather struck.

Arkaroola had been declared a wildlife sanctuary a few years ago. The mountains surrounding the resort were known to hold rich mineral deposits. An initial exploration was far advanced when the government passed an act that prohibited such enterprise. It forces South Australia into millions of dollars in compensation. It was a popular decision and ended the Sprigg's long and exhausting political fight. The Sprigg family owned Arkaroola.

Reginald Sprigg, when he died in 1994, had reached legendary status as a scientist for his unwavering belief in the geological wealth of Australia. He was also an avid conservationist. It resulted in the purchase of Arkaroola, a station in far north in the Flinders Ranges. The property held a pastoral lease. Over time Reg switched the focus from sheep to wildlife. All documented in the book *Rock Star* by Kristin Weidenbach. It was a good read, Emma reflected – quite incredible. She remembered borrowing it from one of her aunts. Today Reg's daughter Margaret, and her brother Doug, ran the resort. He was a keen pilot and used the Arkaroola airstrip to indulge in this hobby. His scenic flights, by all accounts, were spectacular. High above the mountains, Emma mused. Like a massive eagle. That would be fun.

Jake had found the drive interesting. The mountains featured some of the oldest geological formations in the world. Scientists from all over were known to visit. Many a ridge clearly had been formed by one plate of the earth's crust pushing against and over another. It left massive cuts exposed, showing a layered surface of strata. The lines in the rock and its colourings made that clear. The whole landscape was a mixture of reds and brown. Millions of years had weathered the surface and reduced the height of the mountains. The corrosion filled in the valleys. But that idea had lately been disputed. The road twisted through this majesty with bends, straights and creeks. It had not rained for some weeks and the creeks were dry.

'The moment of truth is near,' Jake said. 'What do you reckon?'

Emma felt she had got it right. 'He has been here,' she answered confidently. That brochure in his bedroom and the attraction of this fabulous mountain country made it a certainty. 'Let's see.'

They pulled up at the reception, a low building of cut local stone with a few tables and chairs in front. The place included a shop that offered all sorts for the tourist and camper. Further on a bar and restaurant were available. The reception counter was at the back of an open space.

Emma decided to take the lead. After all, this whole trip had been her idea. It would be best to personalise the inquiry as much as possible.

'We are supposed to meet a friend here. We're not sure though whether he might have moved on. We've been delayed.' A small adjustment of the truth would do no harm, Emma decided.

'Sure,' the lady said. 'What's his surname?'

'Hombrenos.'

Swift typing on the keyboard soon gave the answer. 'Mr. Hombrenos left over a week ago, I'm afraid.' The lady smiled.

That showed she had been right. Emma felt a jolt of excitement, which soon dissipated. That JH no longer was around had also been confirmed.

'Yes. We were wondering about that. Could we have a campsite for the night please? There is no need for power. We wouldn't mind it to be secluded and sheltered against the wind. If possible.' Should they decide to stay for an extra night it wasn't a problem. Campsites here were in the hundreds. That much Emma remembered.

'Would you like to be within walking distance of the amenities, or are you planning to drive up there by car?'

'Car is fine.'

Soon they had a site allocated with a map to show directions. It wasn't far to go. Jake had drifted off towards one of the displays.

They drove through a valley leaving the hill of powered sites to their left. It was best suited to caravans and campers that could withstand strong winds. This was mountain country and always unpredictable. Sand storms blowing in from the deserts beyond were not uncommon. Years ago, if she remembered correctly, Arkaroola had been battered by massive hail. Emma slowly drove the winding track and soon their camp site came in view. It was lovely. Very slightly sloped to allow for rain to run off. With a nice tree and some bushes. The ground was rocky, of course, covered by sparse vegetation and dust. These were the mountains. There were no protruding stones of significance. With rain not expected setting up camp would be a breeze. Just some chairs and a table. The swags could remain in the car till needed.

They spent the rest of the afternoon invigorated by each other, as lovers are. Jake figured that the amenities could be reached fairly quickly by walking up a steep hill and decided to have a look. He shouted down to Emma to bring whatever was needed to have a shower. She found their toiletries and towels easily and soon reached the top of the hill also. A hot shower would be good. Everything in the shower block was clean and comfortable. With Arkaroola totally dependent on water from their own dam guests were asked to limit its use. It had become scarce right now. One big storm with a good run-off and all would be replenished.

Back at camp Emma noted they had not gathered firewood on their journey in. Vegetation in the mountains was sparse, but some dead stuff could have been found. Around there campsite it wasn't much. They were not the first looking for fuel. A fire would be nice though and wood was for sale at the resort. They drove back for a bag of split blocks.

Their meal was similar to the night before. Instead of sausages Emma took two steaks, bought at the butcher in Orroroo, out of the fridge/freezer. Tinned carrots would replace yesterdays' green peas. Jake offered, but Emma didn't mind cooking again. 'You just keep an eye on the fire,' she suggested. 'And get us some beers out of the fridge, please.'

When darkness had set in and they were comfortably seated, Emma asked Jake what his father had been like. She had a good idea, but it was a way of getting Jake to talk about himself. He said that when you are sixteen and your father dies suddenly, you never would know him as you might in adulthood. Nor were you that ready to give much thought to what he had been like. But Jake easily remembered him as great to be with. Obviously, he was clever, but he wasn't proud of it. People liked him and he was a good teacher. Not that he ever taught Jake anything, academic.

'But what did you learn from him as a person? What stands out in your mind?' Emma persisted.

'Not sure,' Jake replied. He had never considered it. 'Probably, that he was quite tolerant and not quickly judgmental. You must give people space, he used to say.'

'You miss him,' Emma said. 'Of course.' It was an observation rather than a probe.

Jake nodded. As a fire always invited to, he stared into it.

Not one for asking many questions himself, Emma concluded, after some time.

'You affect my feelings, Jake, but I don't know that much about you, really.'

Jake looked at her. That would be right. But then, they hadn't spent that much time together. Never like this. Talking about feelings. Emma was stirring his with a whirl. 'Ask away,' he said.

'Have you ever had a girlfriend?' Typical female inquisitiveness. Or was she tempting jealousy perhaps. Wanting to own him absolutely and know about it. Be queen bee? The thoughts confused her, but the question had been put.

'Sure,' Jake revealed. 'One, during my student years.'

'You lived together?'

Jake didn't mind explaining. 'No. I lived at home and she had digs.' He looked at Emma mischievously. 'And now you wish to know whether I slept with her.'

That put her aback. She gazed intently upon the hot embers. 'I never asked that,' Emma mumbled.

'That I know,' Jake replied, a little amused. 'Well, a number of times. It's the kind of thing you do these days when you enjoy someone's company for almost a year. Society talks about sex insistently. It gets to you. Was it anything special? I don't think so. But it was fine.'

Emma didn't move.

'Was I much in love? No. Not anything like what I am feeling for you.'

Emma gave him that look, Jake noticed. He had no way of describing it. A mixture of apology and scrutiny.

'Anyway,' he said, completing the story. 'She left for Europe and it was just as well. We had run our course. I'm actually glad to have told you.'

For a while neither of them spoke. Jake sipped his beer. But then, an eye for an eye, he had his own question. 'And who did you have sex with?'

Emma looked at him, turned scarlet, and was hoping that the darkness hid it. Jake didn't pay her attention trying not to seem aggressive. Fair enough, she thought. I asked for this.

'When I was intoxicated with drink in Paris once,' she said softly. Back at gazing into the fire. 'It was a mistake.'

Jake didn't respond leaving her to mull it over. As a pragmatist he took the news easily. Life could dish up situations like Emma's readily enough.

The guy had known how to work a woman, Emma remembered. Alcohol and charm. She had only herself to blame. He was fun and in no way a Casanova. Paris got to her. She had been on a high after visiting the Louvre. Like what a music concert could do to you. She could have stopped him. But the mood had her curiosity fired up. The guy had been quick in the act. By getting her to want it, she was soon laid. Burning on hormones and aware of her stupid mistake. That was what she told herself, afterwards. She had drifted off not unpleasantly in an intoxicated blur. None of this Jake would ever know, of course.

'Ah well, now we both know,' Emma said ruefully.

The fire flared up in a brief gust of wind.

'Emma.' Jake called for her to face him. 'Don't fret. You're beautiful.'

Her eyes filled up. Damn it. Just like yesterday.

'Let's stay one more night,' Jake suggested,

changing the conversation. 'I don't think JH is awaiting our arrival.'

Not a cloud in the sky the next morning. Emma and Jake talked it over. Whether they could afford money for something special. Neither wishing to put the other in financial difficulty. Whatever the JH situation, they were actually on holiday. Finding funds for a bit of fun would not be a problem, they decided. In the morning, they took a leisurely walk for a few hours and visited an exhibition opposite reception. They splashed out on the four-wheel drive Ridge Top tour. It was expensive but spectacular. They sat on benches bolted to the flatbed of a Toyota that climbed over large rocks and through steep descents into deep valleys. The track ended via a ridge way up at Siller's lookout. It which could accommodate three vehicles. The views were breathtaking. Mountains all round and the flat plain of the eastern desert beyond. The Flinders Ranges ended just north of Arkaroola. Emma had enjoyed the tour years ago, but gladly did so again. For Jake it was a new experience. One day he would own a vehicle that could traverse mountains.

Back at their camp site they crashed down for a nap. Though neither of them did actually fell asleep. It was just great to lie on your back staring into the blue sky with the occasional insect buzzing about. Jake noticed a large bird high up. It easily used the thermal lifts to drift in circles without moving its wings.

Tonight they would look up again. Visit the stars in one of the three observatories of Arkaroola. On a good night, the Arkaroola sky was the clearest in the Southern Hemisphere. Some take-away dinner beforehand would be nice, Emma suggested. The quality of the food was fine. As expected at a high-end tourist destination. They drove up to buy dinner and filled their car with diesel. Let's eat at our camp, Emma suggested. She had come this far to enjoy the bush and the quietness, rather than a heap of tourists.

Their site was not far from the resort. An easy walk for about twenty minutes. They walked to the observatory just before the night fell. Looking through a powerful telescope was incredible. Jake remembered the skies when travelling with Baz through the Simpson Desert. How impressive they were. Yet incomparable to what he was seeing today. Emma also became enchanted by the universe.

Time flew by and soon they were walking back with arms around each other. Emma was resting her head against Jake's shoulder. This nightly walk was the reason why she had suggested not using the car. Jack had a torch, but Emma asked him not to use it. They could see the track well enough. Even though the moon was hidden behind the mountains. With her lover in the outback at night, Emma thought. Walking through a mysterious land. Could it get any better? The bush looked very different now with deep shadows and a ghostly kind of aura.

'You love me Jake, hey?' Emma mumbled.

He grunted some kind of confirmation.

'You think, I'm gorgeous. '

My word he did. But said nothing. He felt her nestle just that little bit firmer into his side.

'Tell me, how gorgeous I am.'

Jake kept his silence. Why couldn't he just be allowed to enjoy their walk together without that request? He had no idea what to say. Life hadn't prepared him for it. He suddenly realised this was not what modernity was about.

'I haven't got the language, Emma,' he admitted, hoping to end their conversation.

She had not expected him to. But felt that having the language would be very good for their loving.

'Ah well, as long as you are convinced of it,' she

conceded.

That would not be a problem.

We must learn that language, Emma decided. Not sure how. The language of Eros, and of love.

PART TWO

10

THE BOAT WAS WHITE and luxurious, built within the last decade. It was held in place by four thick ropes thrown over two bollards. The two long ropes fixed from the back curved into the grey water towards the grassy river bank. Altogether it was a bleak sight. The wide slate-grey river lined by gums and willows in a driving rain. It was just a squall, they were told. But the forecast for the weekend wasn't great. Not that they would lack comforts. This vessel has got everything, Emma thought, like a hotel. Only the restaurant was missing.

JH had won a weekend on a houseboat from a raffle ticket for a worthy cause. Cruising along the Murray River alone didn't appeal. He had decided to find company or otherwise give the ticket away. Without any real friends, the obvious people to invite were his housemates and Jake. They had readily accepted. Spending time on the river would be fun. JH explained that the weekend he had in mind would be the beginning of a holiday for him into the outback, up north. He would travel on from Murray Bridge, where the boat was moored.

After an hour's drive from Adelaide, two cars in convoy, they arrived at the marina Friday afternoon and would leave on Sunday. Provisions were lifted out of the tray of JH's old Toyota pickup with a covering structure of canvas about three feet high. It would be his 'tent' when on holiday. Soon they were installed nicely. Jake braced the rain and undid the heavy ropes while JH had the two powerful outboards pressing the vessel into the embankment. With Jake on board the power was switched into reverse and they made a large curve backward into the centre of the river. From then on it was onward upstream. With the Murray being regulated by a number of locks the flow was limited. The wind swept up small waves and pushed the boat sideways. JH corrected it with the wheel. He stood in the front corner of the living area. A lot of glass all round gave excellent views.

'Cuppa for anyone?' Ruth asked from the kitchen. She had been in two minds whether to come along today. But felt that the time for opting out had passed. That would have been last week at their meeting about the final arrangements. Perhaps she could have conjured up some excuse then. The actual reason for her reluctance she could hardly reveal. It had been felt acutely only after everything was settled, anyway.

The evening had been nice enough. Ruth and Emma's kitchen had a small table that could sit four. Open boxes of delivered pizzas were on the kitchen bench. Help yourself and sit down, Ruth said, handing out a small plates. Beer was in the fridge and also white wine. The bottle of red from JH stood breathing on the sideboard. It promised to be a good night.

The discussion about who would bring what to the boat didn't take long. A weekend was only a short time. Everything besides food was supplied including linen. They would have to pay for the fuel later when a bill arrived in the mail. We'll go the weekend after next then, JH remarked. Jake had written out what was expected of everyone and handed that around. They spent the next half hour engaged in small talk. Until, Emma put a question to JH. Though not a full-on Christian, whatever such a person would be like, she still had a keen interest in her faith. Less perhaps than during her discussions with Joe. But sincere enough. She just didn't think church to be anything special.

'You called yourself a friend of Jesus some time ago,' she reminded JH. 'Different from Christian. Why?'

JH gave them his customary smile, friendly and appreciative.

'I did. There are a number of reasons. First of all, what is a friend? A helpful starting point is the concept of Eros, which we discussed some time ago. Jake wasn't there but he should be familiar with the idea.'

'I'm sorry,' Ruth interrupted. She looked weary. 'I have a busy day tomorrow and a headache right now. Would you excuse me?' She began to make her way from the table to her bedroom. Emma was a little surprised. Ruth never seemed to have headaches, but fair enough. They all made accommodating comments.

'The two most significant manifestations of Eros are love and friendship,' JH continued. 'The lover and the special friend. There is a distinct difference between those two. The lover can be a lover without love being reciprocated. That is painful. The friend cannot be a friend without someone returning the friendship.'

That's true enough, Emma concluded.

JH explained. 'Friendship, at the level of Eros, is

actually rather rare. It involves interaction of a kind that is very self-giving and showing ultimate concern. There are no bodily passions involved. Nor is physical attraction an issue. A good friend is simply just that, someone who deeply cares and seeks to benefit the other person. The lover also cares deeply. But sexual desires are never far away. Whether those are actualised or not. Both lover and friend seek fulfilment by means of someone else. That desire without which life seems incomplete. The manner in which it is achieved though is different for lover and friend.'

'Can you be a lover and a friend?' Jake asked.

'The way in which I have described it, not quite,' JH explained. 'It doesn't mean that lovers can't also be real friends. That would be best. But they would be lovers first and are attracted by each other's looks. You can remain lovers all your lives even when sexual drives begin to wane. Actually you should be. You may insist that in fact you are good friends. That it has served you well through the years. That might well be true. But it comes short of describing the real relationship. If I would suggest to true lovers to get into bed with someone else, they would reject that idea out of hand. They are lovers, who are friendly together. While in the friendship I'm referring to, an expression of Eros, sex with someone else need not be a problem.'

'But it could be,' Emma suggested.

'Sure. It much depends. Human situations are always complicated. People are deep waters.'

'This relates to what Jesus meant, when he called his disciples friends,' Jake wondered. That made sense.

'Yes. Perhaps that is insufficiently understood.' JH raked his fingers through his black hair as if to sharpen his mind. 'Our everyday idea of friendship simply doesn't measure up to what Jesus was referring to. He actually explained his meaning. Nobody has greater love than one who lays down his life for his friends. The designation friend in this context alludes to the summit of human relation when the sexual is irrelevant.'

When neither Jake nor Emma made comment, JH continued.

'Jesus said, that he called them friends because he had completely shared his heart with them. All that he heard from the Father had been passed on. This typically is what a deep friendship entails. Such friends don't harbour secrets. Nor are they reluctant in telling what they are about. What has their passion. Sometimes, that may seem quite crazy. What Jesus was about surely did. But friends will support and hang in there. They will seek to understand and to please. Jesus qualified that the disciples would be his friends, if they did as he was suggesting. It was the benchmark by which they could maintain true friendship. After all, they had been privileged to experience the nature of the Son of God firsthand. They were associates in his mission. He made the point that theirs was not a master/slave situation. They were friends.'

JH stood up, grabbed another slice of pizza from the counter and took a bite chewing it thoughtfully. Jake decided to lift a beer from the fridge.

'Friendship,' JH said after a while, 'originates from the human spirit. Feelings and thoughts will colour it, but the impetus comes from far deeper. Being a friend of God, who is spirit, is immanently possible. One divine Spirit interacting with the human spirit. Always, friends are intimate. It is possible to be intimate with God in spirit. And no-one has a more special place with another than a true friend.'

'A lover could,' Emma said.

'Sure. I should have added: when the sexual is not in play.'

Emma remembered her discussions with Joe about mysticism. 'Mystics are lovers of God,' she said.

JH nodded his head. 'Yes. I'm not suggesting that

the words love and lover shouldn't be used relationally with regard to God. Those words are quite essential. I 'm addressing the meaning in calling myself a Friend of Jesus. That can be best explained in using ideas like Eros and what that is about.'

'Greek mythology comes in handy,' Jake said, mostly to himself.

'Yes. My idea isn't new. St Augustine considered Eros to be the power that drove a person to God. Being mightily attracted might be the better description.'

I should read up more about Eros, Jake reflected. It surely was a most relational concept. He decided to move the conversation along with Emma's original question. 'You're not fond of the word Christian, I understand.'

'Not for me, no,' JH said. 'It's about identification. Of course, I'm a Christian. But that's not precise enough for who I feel to be. Using the right words with yourself about your feelings is important. Friend of Jesus is more accurate.'

'Making others understand the intended meaning of your words is likewise important,' Jake said. Wittgenstein came to mind, a philosopher who had highlighted the ambiguity of language.

'Yes.' JH agreed. 'Not only may the conceptual

meaning of a word be insufficiently understood, but its emotional and intuitive value as well.' He had figured the origin of Jake's comment. Wittgenstein suggested that many experiences cannot ever be put into words well.

Jake smiled. This was fun. Emma sensed she was missing some point here and enjoyed the discussion all the same.

'Talking about Christian,' JH said, 'the meaning of that word, how it is perceived, is a real problem. It hardly describes the believer much more these days than I calling myself a South American. The term Christian has become void of significant meaning. It is seen as a cultural add-on to what life is really about. Recently, the negative history Christian works has become only too obvious. Just read about child abuse and the church. Try explain the true meaning of being Christian facing that. It's depressing.' JH sounded frustrated.

In the silence that followed Emma heard the wailing sound of a siren a few streets down fading away into the distance. It could be police or ambulance.

'So, what now?' she asked after a while. 'We can't turn the clock back.'

'No,' JH admitted. 'Not only has the Church let society down, it has insufficiently supported believers in what really matters. The leadership hardly ever asks how you understand your belief. How you feel about it? Your faith, its meaning and associate emotions. Those intuitive spiritual feelings. The Eros of being attracted to the Lord, someone wonderful, should be the foundation of what you are trying to explain to yourself. But you cannot, for your spiritual ability has not been sufficiently nurtured.'

That was my life before I met Joe, Emma thought. She identified completely with what JH was suggesting.

'So how do you ever become a Friend of Jesus with hurdles like that?' Jake wished to know.

'Not by doing away with church,' JH said. 'Though that is always a temptation. You must become discerning about what you are involved in. Not take all at face value. You are not without information. Every religion consists of core beliefs. Much is written explaining those. It has a cult and a historical tradition. Religion creates feelings. Those can range from passion to just social conveniences. Altogether a religion is a broad spectrum of knowledge, practice and diversity.'

'But a Friend of Jesus is not religious though,' Emma said. 'It's kind of deeper.'

JH had come to appreciate her perceptiveness and nodded in affirmation.

'Well said. But how do you get deeper, as you call it? You must find your passion. Or rather, you must ask God's passion to find you. Ask and you will receive. Pray about it. Once you feel it stirring you on, you turn to God. Always turn to God. And begin to live with a passion for Jesus in the back of your mind. If you're humble, it will guide you well. Avoid being too sure about anything apart from the demands of love. Of the good. Real love needs a passion of heart and a mind of wisdom. Ask for wisdom and you will sense its insights. Let Eros live. Then you may discern the value of in your religious tradition. Where it counts. And you discard the dross.'

JH let this explanation drift between them.

Eros in action – that statement was, Emma thought.

'So you ignore doctrine and tradition,' Jake asked.

'Not really. But you start with your feelings rather than the intellect. Christianity is affective before being descriptive. You reflect on the intrinsic meaning of your faith. Go back to what Jesus said.'

That seemed fair enough. This friendship thing was focused on the Lord in the first place, Emma understood.

'So, as a Friend of Jesus I should learn to talk the language of that friendship,' she suggested. Basically, that was what her discussions with Joe had been about.

'Yes, the language of love,' JH agreed.

'So you pray?' Jake asked.

'Yes. But that can mean many different things. You may begin with words and end up with no words at all. It is called contemplation.'

'So, how do I learn that?' Jake wished to know.

'I can tell you,' Emma said.

Jake gave her an inquisitive look. Emma was full of surprises.

'My friend Joe once taught me.'[3] She felt almost apologetic about it, which was crazy. Why be defensive with a good thing. Perhaps because she hadn't much practised what Joe had introduced her to.

JH smiled. It explained a few things.

'Why don't you, one day.

---

[3] See *Meeting Emma*, Michael J Spyker, AgapeDeum

11

THE RAIN HAD ABATED from a squall, into a steady drizzle from a grey sky. The wet, and a slight fog, gave the river that drenched look. Not at all unattractive, Emma thought. She remembered South Australian artist Mike Barr. He could paint the wet so well. As if by wiping a dry cloth over his picture it would become moist. Emma quite enjoyed the hazy view. The river wide and its banks hidden by reeds and low hanging vegetation. Jake was learning how to steer the boat. It wasn't difficult. Even a child could keep it on course. Any change in direction came gradually.

They had left the marina a few miles downstream from Murray Bridge. That town had not come into view yet. But the large highway bridge on the Adelaide to Melbourne road they had already passed under. It rose up burying its pylons deep into the riverbed. Now I know what that bridge looks like from underneath,

Emma mused. Not that it mattered much. An older bridge had soon appeared. House-boating was fun. With that relaxed feel about it.

The plan was to bypass Murray Bridge, a town they were familiar with. Find a mooring spot for the night further on. Tomorrow they would sail beyond Mannum and then turn back to tie off at that town late afternoon. Mannum had a nice pub on the river known for its decent meals. Makes us get off the boat for a while, Ruth had insisted. No-one had objected.

The first evening Jake cooked on the barbecue that was bolted down onto the foredeck. A platform from which to alight. A houseboat was a boxed structure, over two drifters. It looked like a transportable home with a flat roof. It had a deck aft as well for the generator and gas bottles. From there a staircase the roof allowed its use as a top deck. With some boats that deck included a spa bath. Jake enjoyed cooking with the river lapping below his feet. The wet had a certain attraction and he felt great. Not least, because Emma was absolutely wonderful. She affirmed their relationship without it overtly showing. It was a sensitivity Jake appreciated. Not just for himself, but for everyone's sake.

All went well with Ruth deciding to find her room early. She looks out-of-sorts, Emma thought. Whether the others noticed it was unclear. JH was happy to join in with a game of cards. None of them stayed up late.

In the morning the sky had broken up from a grey blanket into single clouds drifting through scattered patches of blue. A few rain fronts burst down with force. The squalls left as quickly as they arrived. Winds up high were strong. On the river, it was merely a breeze, until a front arrived. Leisurely comfortable, they meandered past wetlands and shacks. Sometimes a high rock wall. Each bend had its surprises. The day flew by and Mannum, which they had passed previously, came in sight earlier than planned. It was mid-afternoon.

They decided on a walk-about. The town had a lot of history. With an interesting main street well up from the river. Window shopping showed many houseboats to be up for sale. Emma concluded that travelling the same stretch of river every time could become boring. On their way back towards the boat JH suggested a beer in the pub. Emma and Ruth declined. They soon reached the gangplank. Through the large glass sliding door and into the boat's living space. It was chilly. Ruth switched on the air-conditioning.

Emma gave her friend a look-over. Something was bugging her. I could do with a glass of red, Ruth said. So, Emma poured two. She might as well join in.

'I'm sorry, Em,' Ruth apologised sitting well back in a soft settee. Her face looked drained. 'I'm having a hard time of it.'

Emma had no idea what Ruth was talking about. Was it her old boyfriend? Ruth had split up with him not long ago. It's no use, she had said. Never quite explaining what that meant.

'Are you missing Paul?' Emma wondered.

'Yes But not that much.' She had sustained that relationship for over a year. Missing it a little was to be expected.

Emma remained silent. Ruth began to talk.

'Modernity sucks,' she began to explain. 'You try to connect with another person. To fill the aloneness you experience. And you end up more guilt ridden and more anxious than when you were on your own.'

'What happened?' Emma asked.

'What happened? Just everything and nothing.' Ruth threw half a glass full back down her throat. 'You try, and it all ends up being a lie. Perhaps.'

Emma waited.

'You love one-another, right! That's what it's called. You really dig the other person. And the best way to show it, you can guess. It's sex. No sex - no love! That's so very obvious to modern society. You never stop reading about it. All that clever talk. And where does it lead? You are just being sexed in the name of love. You sense that's not what love is really about. But apart from the moralisers, and what would they know about love, nobody will ever tell you differently.'

Emma didn't think it was quite that bad. Ruth was hurting.

'After all. We're liberated from taboos, aren't we? No inhibitions in advanced societies. We're free. The old Victorian mores are gone. So here's how it goes. All with good intentions.'

Ruth poured herself another glass.

'After a number of dates you have to *give*. If you don't, at first, well, that's okay. But every time at the end of a good evening together the expectation increases. The pressure mounts. And you tell yourself come-on, don't be such a prude. And Paul is a nice guy. I know. But he's modern. And, of course – a guy.'

He was definitely that, Emma agreed quietly. Nice and modern.

'So, of course, you give. Not reluctantly, I must

add. I quite enjoyed sex,' Ruth said. 'And I'm not perturbed about being naked. That's never a problem. Not that we ended up in bed every time. I tried to avoid that.'

Ruth had no need to be perturbed about her body, Emma thought. She just had that figure every guy wants.

'Sure. Sex may be fun. But to me it remained a kind of empty fun,' Ruth continued. 'You feel there should be more to it. But you cannot find that. I found that Paul seemed more worried about technique than anything else. Whether he was measuring up to what good sex is supposedly about. I considered joining that bandwagon, and tried. But it's a dead end. You become more fixated with procedure than with the other person. Wow, isn't accomplished sex fun! So they make you believe. You worry so much about technical competence, you might even begin to fake your orgasms. I've never fallen that low. Orgasms are overrated anyway,' Ruth suggested. 'But it's great.'

Emma began to understand where her friend was heading. It was important not to interrupt.

'And then you're in a bind. Sex becomes a problem. Your partner is working hard at being up-to-scratch and you begin to feel like just a receptacle for his efforts. You become pissed off with the whole affair.'

Ruth wiped away her tears. 'And then you call off the relationship with a perfectly good man. You just can't hack it anymore. That insecurity of being a woman. Of having to measure up when you just want to be yourself. And you know. If Paul and I had been able to talk it through, I would have been okay. But we couldn't really. I know, that he would have become defensive. Kind of miffed. I would have misunderstood the whole shebang. Wasn't he trying to help us get the best out of sex? What's wrong with that? I don't think he knows what intimacy, some real loving, is about. Neither do I. But I've got an idea about it. A sense of what was lacking.'

Emma, not wanting to utter platitudes, was lost for words. She had never known this about her friend.

'So,' Ruth continued, 'I break it all up. And why? Because the modern guy is so insecure that he cannot tell you what he really feels for you. Or doesn't feel. So you don't know. I don't want a lasting relationship with that uncertainty. How can I know whether Paul is the one, if intimate intercourse is a problem? What a mess!'

Emma took note of this and thought of Jake. Ruth just sat back all wound up. She seemed not to have finished her story though.

'But the problem is deeper than that I now know.

Paul and I never burned for each other as whole people. Modern people don't expect that in life – no burning beyond sex. We were so suited everyone said. Visually attractive, educationally compatible, you name it. Enough money to enjoy ourselves and thinking that's tops.'

Ruth wiped away more tears. Emma remained silent.

'Our relationship ran out of steam. And I called it off. Perhaps I gave up on a good man. Perhaps, I haven't.'

Ruth was calming down a little. Talking about her problems helped.

'So, now I feel guilty without really knowing why. I'm anxious without understanding the reason. In simple terms, I have, and I am, fucked up.'

'I'm sorry, Ruth,' Emma said. Her friend was too harsh on herself. But it would be of no use mentioning it right now.

'Thanks. But that isn't the end of the story.' Ruth had a flat voice. She sat looking at the ceiling and for while didn't speak. Considering what she was to say.

'You know that talk about Eros. Some time ago, when JH explained it.'

Emma knew full well.

'I felt like being hit in the gut. It came from nowhere. JH explained exactly what I'm looking for.'

There would be more, Emma figured, and there was. Ruth sat back not saying another word. She gazing out of the window now towards the riverbank. A realisation began to dawn on Emma. One that would explain much.

'Not JH, Ruth?' she asked gently.

Her friend's look confirmed it. Ruth had a crush on him. Life could be so unfair, Emma thought.

'It won't work, Ruth.'

'I know.' Ruth stared at a weeping willow far away. 'All because of fucking Eva,' she added hoarsely – after a while.

Emma remained silent.

'That's not fair,' Ruth acknowledged. 'I shouldn't have said that. But what am I to do?'

'When did you realise this?' Emma asked.

'Not long ago. Not for certain that is. I shouldn't have come on this trip.'

'You think you can cope?'

'Yes, I'll cope. I will have to.'

They sat together in silence. Ruth had calmed down. Emma felt kind of punch-drunk. But she had a thought.

'Are you perhaps projecting on JH what you found missing with Paul?' she asked.

'That has crossed my mind,' Ruth admitted. 'I don't know. Time will tell. It doesn't change how I feel though.'

No, it wouldn't do that, Emma understood.

'At least, JH will be off on holidays tomorrow,' Ruth observed. 'That will help.'

Matters might have settled down when JH returned, Emma hoped. But who could tell with Eros?

'I should be okay, Em,' Ruth assured her best friend. 'Thanks for listening. It helps.'

'Will you be alright for that dinner in the pub?'

'Sure. Just wash my face. Be as good as new. Don't worry, I'll manage. I feel better already.' Ruth got up and made for the shower cubicle. Emma's eyes followed her all the way.

Soon footsteps could be heard on the gangplank.

.

12

THE DINNER AT THE PUB had been pleasant. Emma noticed that Ruth enjoyed it. Talking about her feelings must have helped. However, as soon as they arrived back at the boat, Ruth excused herself and went to bed. Emma had been expecting it. The others dropped themselves into comfortable chairs. It was the kind of evening in which you just relaxed. Allowed the time to drift away. Except that Jake, always ready for ideas, reminded JH of a yet undiscussed topic.

'You have thoughts on deconstructing the Gospel,' he said. 'Are you okay with talking about that?'

'That's not the word I would use,' JH chuckled. 'It's a refocusing.'

Jake shrugged his shoulders. Whatever it should be, it had his attention.

JH gathered his thoughts. This talk had to be easy

going. It was that kind of evening.

'When I use the word refocusing for the Gospel, it means two things. Firstly, being able to explain what the Gospel tells us. From beginning to end, leaving nothing and adding nothing. Getting the essence of it.'

'You sound as if that's not really known,' Jake said.

'Just ask someone. You'll be surprised. Usually it's incomplete.'

JH stopped for a moment.

'Secondly, the Gospel is not just a story. There is a spiritual dynamic to it. That dynamic is affective. It has a feeling component.'

'You mean it involves your feelings for Jesus,' Emma suggested. That's what it sounded like.

'Exactly. The Gospel must come alive. It cannot apart from Jesus.'

That statement hung in the air.

'We're back at the Friend of Jesus idea,' Jake said.

'Yes.' JH smiled. 'But let's sidestep for a moment and consider mindfulness. That popular modern concept. It tells us something.'

'That people see themselves as spiritual.' Jake once had a discussion about it with a uni friend.

'Perhaps. It depends. More correctly, people feel the need to focus more on being. They are so busy with doing all day and experience the downside of that. The idea of mindfulness has entered society via the Eastern religions.'

'So it is actually a spiritual concept,' Emma asked.

'Yes. But originally broader than how our society uses it. In Buddhism it is called *smrti*. It has a moral side to it which is not how we understand it.'

JH is a mine of information, Emma thought.

'Psychology has taken to the idea in a major way,' he continued. 'It found two ways in which mindfulness can be helpful. First, a cognitive approach in which you focus your attention the now. Not letting all sorts of issues clutter your mind. Then also an affective one that aims for relaxation through feeling good. Both, actually, are easily found in Christian spirituality.'

Like a day of Holy Leisure, Emma remembered. She should try that again one day. It had been rather nice.

'There is a difference between *smrti* mindfulness and the Christian version though. In Buddhism your focus is on pure being. The notion of a personal self is foreign to Buddhist belief. In our western culture the self is very real. Modern mindfulness aims at gaining benefit for that self. Psychology does so by teaching you mental control and relaxation. Christian spirituality however takes it further. It adds a divinely relational aspect to mindfulness. And that relating is personal.'

'Your Friend of Jesus idea,' Jake reiterated. 'The Gospel cannot be truly meaningful, if you're not that kind of friend. Is that what refocusing means?'

Jake's ability to zero in no longer surprised JH. Both his companions were attentive. He saw it as a mark of respect and it pleased him.

'Yes. The Gospel easily becomes disconnected from Jesus relationally. A believer soon finds out what to know and do. How to live in a Christian way. But befriending Jesus, making him a real friend, is not taught. Or even suggested.'

'So, we're missing out,' said Emma.

'Yes. And not just us. Jesus as well.'

'I wouldn't mind a cup of tea,' Jake said. 'Anyone interested?' He went to put the kettle on.

Soon the tea was served. Everyone engaged with their thoughts. After a while Jake made an observation.

'It's interesting, really. Society is reaching out for the benefits of mindfulness and Christians ignore it. While they could benefit the most. Myself included.'

JH had a twinkle in his eyes. He said nothing.

'Perhaps because Buddhist mindfulness involves

just yourself,' Emma suggested. 'That makes it attractive to people. Coming to rest completely self-focused.'

Trust Emma, Jake thought. Walking into that pub looking for her was the best thing he had ever done. Building up his courage beforehand.

'It's egocentric,' he said.

'It's strange though reaching out to someone you cannot see,' Emma continued. 'When it is meant to be meaningful and you have little idea how.'

That time in her bedroom, during her discussions with Joe, when suddenly she had felt the Lord's presence so distinctly, flashed through her mind. It had helped her in accepting that he was always near. Even then, that sense had soon dissipated in the bustle of living. But at least she has an experience to remember.

'That is a problem,' JH admitted. 'But a poor excuse.'

'It's just human nature,' Jake observed. 'Too busy.'

'Then why is mindfulness so popular? If nobody has time for it,' JH asked. 'I feel, it's more that Christians are not aware of their options. The church gives the idea that its communal happenings are sufficient. It should wake up to its possibilities.'

'And when it doesn't,' Emma asked. 'What do I do? Many Christians don't even go to church anymore.'

'True,' JH agreed. 'But let's not get stuck with that problem right now. One thing that helps in feeling like a Friend of Jesus is your vocabulary.'

Both Jake and Emma looked nonplussed. Are we back at Wittgenstein again, Jake wondered.

'Philosophy of late has insisted that the meaning of words is ambiguous. What really are they referring to? It might differ depending on the person. That is, if you wish to be exact about a word,' JH said.

So it is Wittgenstein, Jake concluded.

'But the problem with being a Friend of Jesus is, that we often don't use the words available to us. Those that facilitate the relationship best. Not spoken words per se. It could be words used in our mind.'

'We don't speak a relational language. That's what you mean,' Emma said.

'Yes,' JH agreed. 'We use certain words far less than we might. We may not know their meaning sufficiently either. Their precise meaning, that is. But also, we hardly engage with the depth of their affective meaning. There is more to words than just the cognitive.'

Philosophy had long caught up with that idea, Jake knew. That words can have a feeling attachment. 'What words are you talking about,' he asked.

'An obviously affective one is love. It means little unless you can bring a feeling to it. That's no different with a love for Jesus.'

'But as Emma mentioned, to love someone you can't see is rather difficult,' Jake observed.

'That's not really true though,' Emma said. 'Not with Jesus. He can make you feel that love.' It's what it had felt like in that evening in her room

'Yes, very true.' JH liked that comment. 'The kinds of words I am referring to, use them sincerely, and the Lord will help you feel their meaning. Beyond what your soul is capable of on its own. But it will be subtle. Don't expect goose bumps and believe in what you sense.'

'But you have to use the words first.' Jake saw the point.

'What words do you have in mind?' Emma asked.

'Words that allow for affectivity. There are quite a few. Some allow even more for it than you think. Take the word grace. It means more than a just benevolent blessing. Grace also means being empowered by God. It is an enablement. It makes you capable. Knowing that makes you feel different about the word. It's a great word to experience together with Jesus.'

'That's your point,' Jake said. 'When our language is vibrant with meaning, a relationship deepens out. That would be true generally.'

'Very much so.'

I must remember that, Jake thought. And felt uneasy right away. Verbalising his feelings didn't come naturally to him.

'There are lots of suitable words in relating to Jesus,' JH continued. 'Like: trust, gratefulness, faith, adoration, amazement, confidence, hope and others. Purposefully using those with feeling towards Jesus builds a friendship. As Emma said, he will help you.'

'It's a kind of technique,' Jake offered.

'If you like. More a set approach.'

'So, refocusing means learning to speak the language of love,' Emma said. 'A language worthy of God.'

He couldn't have said it better himself, JH thought.

'Precisely. And for that language to be worthy, as you called it, knowing the core ideas of God's work helps. It helps you to speak more purposefully with wonder and joy.'

'Which is the second aspect of your refocusing,' Jake said. 'The plan of God.' He had kept that in mind.

'Yes,' JH agreed. 'There is no time to discuss that. The most important is, that I'm aware of the endgame of God.'

'My father was adamant about that.' Jake felt a pang of regret.

'He would have been a spiritual man,' JH affirmed.

He had been. Not that Jake ever really got that idea. Dad had been as normal as anyone. Very grounded.

'Liam was right,' JH said. 'Without appreciation of our heavenly future, and that of the whole universe, the Gospel cannot work its full magic on you. You remain overly focused on the now. God makes less sense.'

'You mean, it limits our language with God,' Emma asked.

'What you don't think about, you won't talk about. Simple as that. Nor will you have feelings for it. I cannot be grateful for what I don't give attention to. Or may not know.'

'So, the Gospel can only touch my emotions to the extent that it is part of my awareness.' It was obvious, but Jake liked it, these nuances.

'Yes,' JH agreed. 'But there is another side to this as well. I may have heard the Gospel properly and then it becomes too embellished with information of secondary importance. I may no longer discern the significance of what really matters.'

'You won't see the forest for the trees kind of thing,' Jake suggested.

JH nodded.

'And that's your beef with the church?' Jake had long figured that. The word refocusing said as much.

'Yes. The essential Gospel is drowning in dogma and ritual. It is not central to church expression. As I said before. Ask a Christian to tell it to you and see how they fare. Few will tell the Gospel to a friend simply and in full. (See Appendix)

'So, what would you describe a Friend of Jesus to be like?' Emma asked.

Trust Emma, JH thought. It was a good question. He had never summed it up for himself really and would best be careful.

'Nothing special. Just an ordinary person. Good to be with and not overly spiritual. More like, supernaturally natural,' JH began.

'The difference is in what doesn't show openly. It is someone, who is aware of Christ all the time. Relates to him without reservation. Like a friend would.'

JH paused for a moment.

'There is no burden of obligation, but the pleasure of doing your best. Life isn't any easier, but meaningful. A Friend of Jesus takes time for this friendship, knows the Gospel, and speaks the language of love.'

Silence settled.

A gust of wind struck the houseboat.

'Thanks, JH,' Emma said.

His name is actually Jesus, she remembered.

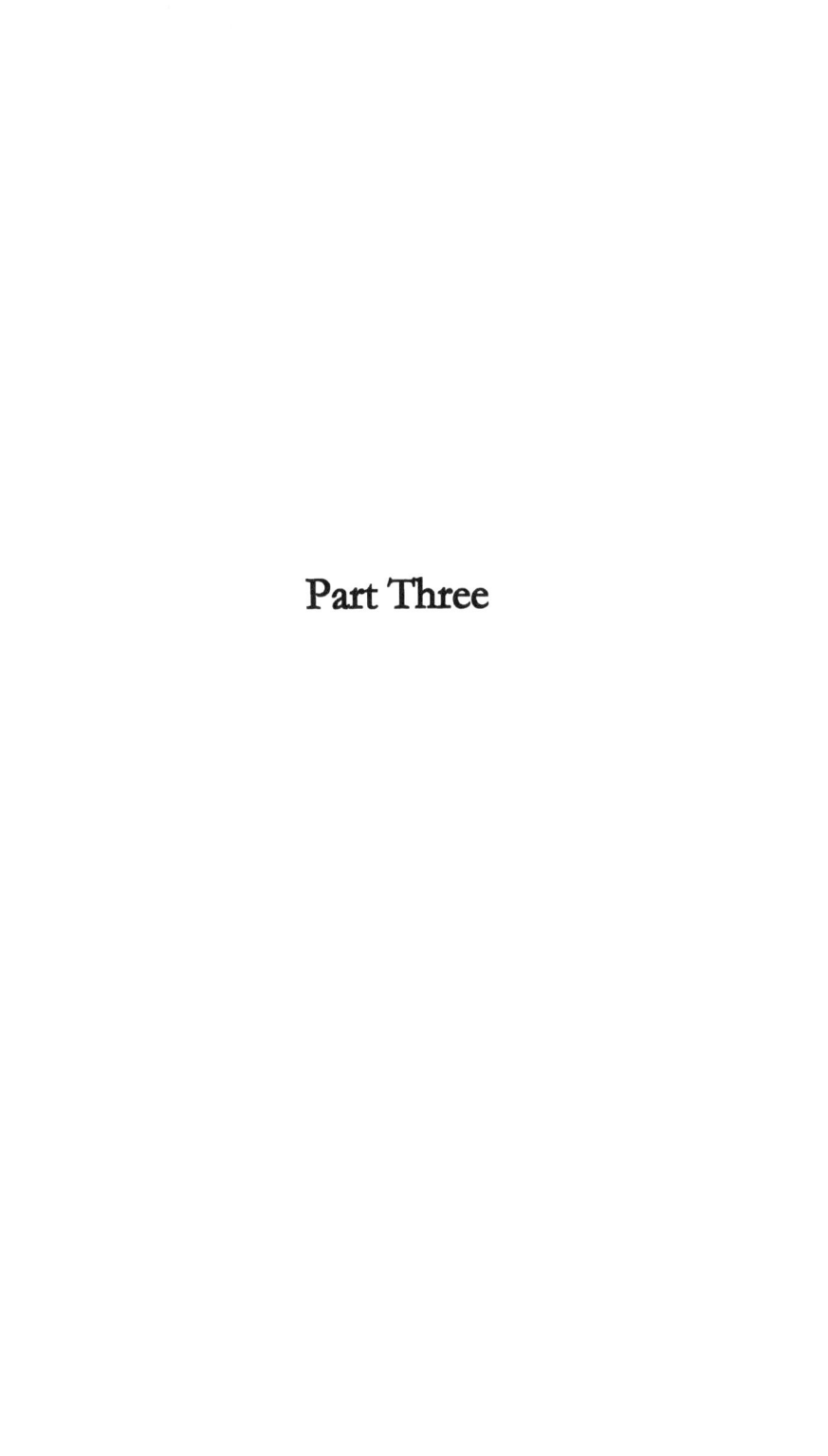

Part Three

13

THE DIRT ROAD out was less well maintained than the one they had taken into Arkaroola. They were travelling in a southern direction towards Blinman. A wide creek bed came in view and the Discovery easily negotiated its banks. It was one of those ancient flash flood waterways that could fill up enormously and fast. A golden rule was not to set up camp in a creek bed. Wet weather upstream could bring on a powerful surge of water and endanger your life. You would have no idea that it was raining far away. Jake settled the car at an easy speed of forty miles. The suspension handled the corrugated road surface with ease, which might lessen your concentration. A keen eye remained necessary in avoiding potential pitfalls ahead. Roads out back, even when maintained, could deteriorate quickly.

'You might have heard from him by now,' Jake

said. 'He could have left a message on your phone.'

'Perhaps he's out of range,' Emma responded. In all honesty, she was hardly concerned anymore. She even wondered whether the JH situation had been an excuse for a holiday with Jake out bush.

'Perhaps the phone lost power. He may not have a car charger,' Jake suggested.

'Who knows,' Emma said. She was quite happy to let the situation be. 'He may have come home already,' she offered. 'JH is a loner. Won't contact anyone soon.'

'If he's home, Ruth would have let you know.'

'Ruth is away for a fortnight,' Emma said. 'There's nobody home.' Ruth was visiting her parents in Mildura. Then would follow on to Melbourne and catch up with friends.

Jake took that information without comment.

'Should we give up and drive straight home then?' Emma asked.

'Not likely,' Jake grinned. Adelaide could wait as far as he was concerned.

'We'll check at Blinman. Ask whether he has passed through. Then we can make up our minds.'

Once out of the mountains, the road travelled through rather flat and uninteresting country but with a proper desert feel. Sparse low vegetation drawing life from a rocky ground made for a monotonous landscape. But it had its own beauty. Emma just loved the open space, the feeling of being in the middle of nowhere. It nourished her soul. Perhaps the Desert Fathers and Mothers in Egypt, a few hundred years after Christ, would have lived in similar surrounds. She reminded herself once more to contact Joe sometime soon. Have a coffee together, as they had done so often before. Emma felt a little guilty that she had never touched base with him after her return from Europe. It would be good to see Joe again.

Eventually, they took a right turn. West, and back into the mountains. The road became rough. Blinman, a copper mine town of old, would not be far away now. The working mine had long been closed. It had become as a tourist attraction. Blinman was the most northern town in the Flinders Ranges that could be reached from the south over bitumen roads. Under the hour, they pulled up in front of the Blinman Hotel. It dated from 1869 and had been modernised not long ago. Let's take a walk and stretch our legs, Emma suggested.

Blinman was one street enclosed by mountains. A few old buildings had a history reaching back into the later eighteen hundreds. Blinman included cottages, a school, police station, store, post office and a library. There was a yard with a few camels not far from the hotel. Jake took Emma's hand as they strolled along. Passing a cottages that had been converted into a coffee shop, they decided to take a break. A coffee would be good and they could ask after JH. Might strike lucky. The lady was kind, but could not remember serving a South American man with a scar on his cheek. Try the hotel, she suggested, most tourists would visit there.

The bar was nice, Emma thought. Nicer than the one she worked at home. Having come this far, it would be foolish not to ask about JH, once again. The man behind the counter looked nonplussed. He called in a woman from the other end. Oh, yes, she said, about a week ago. She well remembered it. Pay-dirt, Emma thought. The woman seemed to have taken a shine to JH. She knew to tell them that he had asked about the Nuccaleena ruins up north, an old mine site. Whether you could camp there.

That was good news with obvious implications. They would travel on to Nuccaleena.

'Let's have an early lunch first,' Jake suggested. 'In this pub.' Emma thought it an excellent idea.

The drive to Nuccaleena started off on a good dirt road that wound through the mountains towards Glass Gorge. Eventually they hit a turn-off to the right over a cattle grid onto land of the Moolooloo sheep station It included Nuccaleena. Soon the way to the old mine took a left turn off the main drive to the station's homestead. They had to tackle about ten miles over a rocky track and washouts. A number of gum-lined creeks had to be crossed. It was careful going but fun, Emma thought. She did the driving. It reminded her of those camping holidays. When Dad had allowed her to have a go. You can drive back, if you like, she told Jake, who grunted some response. Ever the talkative companion, Emma mused. She didn't mind.

From a brochure picked up at Blinman they learned that the Nuccaleena mine was established by William Finke in the mid 1850's. It quickly expanded before closing down just as fast, in the late 1860's. Digging up copper had become uneconomical. A good number of buildings had been built out of local stone. The ruins clearly outlined a large set-up. Just before reaching the mine, and the final creek to cross, the remains of the Tom O'Shanter Bushmans Hotel could be seen. On a hill to their left. Many a miner would have walked there seeking to drown his sorrows, Emma figured. Life had been hard in those days. They drove on the uneven creek bed for a short while avoiding large boulders and climbed up a steep embankment. Over a hill, and the mine came in sight. And so did JH's old Toyota, completely deserted. Emma hit the brakes in surprise. 'Wow,' said Jake, equally nonplussed.

Emma parked the Discovery close in. Jake tried the doors of the Toyota which were locked. A glance inside through the windows told them that the cabin was empty apart from a travel map. He got on his knees to look under the chassis. But having no great knowledge of cars could see nothing wrong. Obviously the vehicle had broken down. Why otherwise abandon it here in this wild place. Emma decided to zip open the canvas canopy over the tray. That told them more. JH had taken the minimum in necessary belongings with, but left all else. They found a blow-up mattress, a folding chair and table plus a small gas cooker. The two water containers were almost empty. A cushion lay discarded in one corner. A plastic bag with rubbish tightly tied up in another. There seemed a fair bit of waste in it. A plastic box for provisions had little left to show. JH must have stayed here for a while. A few days at least.

Jake walked to where JH may have camped and

found the remnants of a fire. The embers were no longer hot. But it might be recent. Not that Jake could really tell. The ash, whatever was left of it, had not been rained out.

'What now?' Emma wondered. 'At least we know he has been here.'

'His car must have broken down,' Jake concluded. 'He must have camped here till some visitors came to the rescue.'

Emma looked at the mine site in the distance. It was quite a spectacle. This place would have been buzzing with people in days gone by.

'We could camp here tonight,' Jake suggested.

'We could,' Emma agreed. 'But I can't. Must know what happened.' There was no arguing about it.

Jake looked at her carefully and understood. That was Emma. Spontaneous and insistent in what she felt was necessary. He shrugged his shoulders.

'Let's find out at the homestead,' Emma said. 'They might know something.'

'Sure,' Jake agreed. It wasn't far and they had plenty of time before sundown.

'You drive.' Emma handed him the car keys.

Moolooloo Homestead had joined the tourist trend now popular with farmers as extra income. Like the farm at Beltana, they offered accommodation. When they pulled up, it was obvious that guests were well catered for. While Jake and Emma made their way to reception, the farmer crossed the yard. He was in his mid-thirties, not much older than they, Emma guessed. Jovial, but reserved. Typical the farmer's type. At least of the kind that was sociable. She had known a fair few during her youth. That the man was rather young surprised her. Many farmers were older. They had difficulty in keeping their children on the land. Definitely so once they had been educated in the cities. The bush could not compete with that.

'G'day,' he greeted them. 'You're looking for a place to stay?'

'Yes,' Emma said. They would not travel on from here this time of day.

'Camping or a cabin?' He saw the Discovery. It was rather expensive for two young people. But said little about the preferred accommodation.

'Camping,' Jake said.

'Not a problem. Just follow me to the office.'

'Could I ask you a question first, please?' Emma interrupted.

'Sure.' She looked country this girl, and nice too. Often you could tell, the farmer knew. Something about them. Not the guy though. But he was a lucky fellow. That much was obvious.

'We found a friend's car abandoned at Nuccaleena. Do you know anything about that?'

The farmer's face turned into a broad grin. 'You mean JH. He's a friend of yours?'

Emma's heart missed a beat. Bingo, they would get their answer. She nodded.

'JH was dropped off here by other tourists. He must have stayed at Nuccaleena for a few days. I visit sort of once a week there, which isn't often. There's enough to do here that comes first. His car made serious noises and refused to travel on. Too expensive for him to have fixed, JH told me. It's an old car.'

'Where is he now?' Jake asked.

'On his way to Sydney, I would think.'

Emma must have shown a stunned look on her face. The farmer grinned again and explained.

'He told me, I would be welcome to the car. Those Toyotas are common and real farm handies. It may not be that costly to get the car right. Not when you're local and somewhat of a mechanic.'

Which all farmers are, Emma knew.

'So, we made a deal. He wanted to go to Sydney. I was about to travel to Peterborough soon to buy a ram. That's a railway town down south, as you would know. The train to Sydney passes there twice a week. I dropped him off a few days ago. He's capable alright. Gave me a hand around the place. Nice guy. I just haven't picked the car up yet with the tractor.'

Typical JH, Emma thought. Her eyes were welling up. A real nomad and she would never see him again. She nodded her head in understanding. 'Thanks,' she said.

'Look,' the farmer continued, not unawares of how that news hit Emma. 'I'll give you a nice campsite and being friends of JH coming all this way looking for him, you can stay there for free as long as you like.'

'Thanks,' Emma said once more, making an effort to speak clearly. 'Just for one night.'

Jake had started their customary fire, the last one of their holiday He would prepare a meal. Emma had become withdrawn since the news about JH. Jake understood grief well. For that was what Emma was feeling. About the knowledge that she wouldn't see JH again. Jake was happy to have known him, but felt little affected by his moving on.

They ate in silence while the darkness fell in. Emma found some solace in the beautiful night. Once again with a clear sky. She warmed her glass of red with her hands and sipped thoughtfully. Feeling melancholy, she had no wish for talking. Jake, the quiet type, didn't mind. There wasn't much he could do right now to lift her spirit. At least, he didn't think so.

'You love me, Jake, hey?' Emma said eventually.

'Yes.' It was all he felt to say.

'I love you too,' Emma said. The words hung about in the darkness.

'You know,' she continued, 'the love God feels for us is way more than we can feel for each other. Isn't that incredible?'

Jake didn't answer. This was unexpected.

Emma hardly noticed and asked him what she had been wondering about.

'All I want to know Jake is your reaction to that Friend of Jesus idea of JH.'

Jake took his time with. He had actually thought about that. In taking a philosophical approach to life, was Jesus important? That was really the question, Emma was asking.

'JH reminded me a lot of my dad. They would have got on famously. My dad was a Friend of Jesus, for sure.'

'And you?'

'I'll try. I love my dad. It would make him happy.' Jake sounded forlorn and was now feeling sad as well.

Emma looked at him and stood up. 'Hold me, Jake, please.'

Slowly he came out of his chair and stood before her.

'You'll never leave me, hey,' she said looking up.

'Never.' His eyes were searching for hers.

What a strong face, Emma thought. She began to cry her heart out on his shoulder. From sadness and joy. How had she ever found this man?

All Jake did was hug her in tight. He had no idea what to say and just stroked her head.

'Oh, Jake,' Emma mumbled a few times.

14

EMMA WALKED through her front door after an afternoon shift in the pub. She had invited Jake for a meal that evening and carried a bag of groceries. It's amazing how quickly life settles back into routine, she thought. Finding JH's car seemed now ages ago. Though they had arrived back only last weekend. It was Wednesday today and her evening off. When they had separated at Jake's place after the long drive, she had invited him for dinner. With the comment that he could then properly tell her how gorgeous she was. Tongue in cheek that. They had briefly kissed. Making an early start, and with only a short stop-over at her mother's, they had managed to get back to Adelaide in one day. Emma had promised her mum that soon she would come up for a while. She'd better not forget. That would be completely unfair.

Emma was alone. Ruth would be back on Sunday. Emma switched on the gas heater for warmth and began making preparations in the kitchen. It would be the first time she was meeting Jake again after their adventure. She was really looking forward to it. In fact, she could hardly wait. Love did strange things to you. Or was it Eros perhaps? Emma didn't care what you called it. She was just enthralled with the emotions. Clearly, Jake would feel the same. Just as well. Imagine being in love and someone was not interested. Poor Ruth, Emma thought.

Soon there was a knock. Jake found the door unlocked and walked in. Please lock up behind you, Emma shouted from the kitchen. He arrived with open arms holding a bottle of wine. Eventually, Emma disentangled herself reluctantly from his embrace. She needed to cook a meal. Jake's comment that he'd happily just eat her, was ignored with a smile. Keep control, girl, she told herself. Jake settled at the kitchen table and Emma threw some pasta into boiling water. She was cooking a marinara with fresh prawns and calamari from the fish shop. A tangy sauce to give it some spice and all would be well.

'Have you heard from JH?' Jake asked.

'A postcard, on the dresser. Feel free to read it.'

The card had been waiting for her when she arrived home. The postmark showed Peterborough. It explained what they already knew. A cheque for one month's rent and fuel for the houseboat was included.

'It doesn't explain much about him moving on that suddenly,' Jake commented.

'No. But I know the reason.' Emma dropped the fish into a red hot pan for a quick stir fry. She would add a dash of marinating sauce soon.

'And that is?'

Emma finished with the fish before she replied. The pasta was ready also. Jake waited patiently. He was not inquisitive by nature. Except when something had his real interest.

'Ruth has a crush on him,' Emma said. 'Not that she expected anything.'

'Ah. And JH noticed,' Jake concluded.

'He must have.' Jake didn't know about Eva, nor would Emma ever tell him. 'He must have felt it best to move on.'

'Fair enough.'

'He might have moved soon anyway,' Emma said. 'That breakdown simply sped matters up. Just get me two plates from the bottom of that cupboard, will you?'

Emma pointed it out. She extracted hot pasta sauce from the microwave.

Jake placed the plates on the table. The marinara was dished up in seconds. It smelled great. During the meal Emma asked after Sandy, Jake's mother. She would like you to come over soon, Jake explained. Emma would be happy to. They made small-talk until after dinner. Then Jake surprised her with a lopsided grin on his face.

'I now know how gorgeous you are,' he offered.

Emma's heart skipped a beat. The kitchen seemed hot, suddenly. She understood what he was referring to. 'You found the language,' she said, beginning to feel distinctly stirred.

'Yes.' Jake forced himself to stay calm. I'll never be good at this, he thought.

'And?'

He raised his glass of red in a toast. 'How delicious is your love, more delicious than wine.' He said it slightly struggling.

Emma was taken aback. Where did this come from? But she liked it – a lot.

'You ravish my heart with a single one of your glances.' Jake was becoming more confident and looked at Emma intently. She began to blush.

'Your lips are a scarlet thread and your words enchanting.'

Emma looked away, shaking her head as if to clear a fog. This was getting to her.

'How beautiful you are, my beloved, how beautiful you are!' Jake was beginning to enjoy this. More so because he meant what he said. Of course, he couldn't have come up with it all by himself – not without some help..

'Where does all this come from?' Emma asked hoarsely. Surely, Jake hadn't dreamt it up. Suddenly, she had an idea. 'You bugger. It's the Song of Solomon, isn't it?'

Jake grinned. 'Would you like to hear some more?' Without waiting for a reply, he continued. 'Who are you arising like the dawn, fair as the moon, resplendent as the sun?'

'Stop it, Jake,' Emma mumbled feebly. She tried not to giggle. This was playing havoc with her hormones.

'But you wanted me to tell you how gorgeous you are?' he reminded her.

'Yes, I know,' she had to admit.

'The curve of your thighs is like the curve of a necklace, work of a master hand,' he declared. 'Your neck is an ivory tower. May your breast be clusters of grapes, your breath sweet-scented as apples, and your palate like sweet wine.' It had taken him some time to memorise all this.

Emma grabbed the edge of the table with both hands. Her head was spinning.

'And you know,' Jake said softly, 'that's just how I feel.'

'You've found the language of love,' Emma said after some time. She calmed herself down. 'I had no idea, what it could do to me.'

For a while she just sat there, as if in a trance. Jake let it be, himself taken up in the moment.

'And what am I like to you then,' he asked. 'Also gorgeous?'

That was not difficult at all. Often she had made up sentences in her mind.

'You stand like a Nordic god of the Danes,' she began. She knew that Jake's mother had Danish ancestry.

Jake recognised the reference and was pleased. Not that it could arouse him more than he was already.

'Your eyes are crystal azure. Blue as a clear ocean,' Emma continued. 'You are like a stallion with a fair mane, an eagle in flight.'

Now it was Jake's turn to become embarrassed. This sounded way better than he felt to be true.

'A swift arrow you are my love, a harbour in storms.' Emma began to get a feel for it, this Solomon stuff. She was now making it up spontaneously. 'You are as nectar to my heart, strong drink to my passions.'

Jake was stunned. Emma was surprised herself. This language was getting under her skin.

Jake had a final quote. He might as well use it.

'I have love no flood can quench, no torrent can drown.'

It no longer sounded as contrived as when he had put it to memory. In his ignorance he had learned these sentences mostly for fun. To show Emma that he could tell her how gorgeous she was after all. But that fun had never arrived. His very first words had deeply affected her. So that was how language worked. If you used its power properly.

Emma looked at her lover with big eyes. He was adorable. There was no escaping now and the thought never came to mind.

'Hey, Jake,' she said with a smile. 'You think, you can tell me how gorgeous I am in your own words?'

Jake nodded his head. He would try, even though he felt tired now. As he was searching for what to say next, Emma spoke.

'Not in this kitchen,' she said softly. 'Come to my room.'

She stood up to lead the way.

APPENDIX

GOD TALK

What I told my friend

A friend and I were having a yarn over a cup of coffee. The opportunity arose to explain what the Gospel is about. As Christians we know the Good News. But often in the bits and pieces that come to us over time. The following is what I told my friend in a non-religious way (headings excluded).

Spiritual but not religious

Everyone is spiritual by nature. What does that mean?

Ask anyone, and they will consider themselves as having a spirit. They will accept that the idea of spirit extends beyond physical limitations. It can reach out from one person to another. Like expressions of empathy or anger. Religion holds that a person's spirit also extends into a spiritual realm beyond the natural. That realm is not neutral though. Like our world, it struggles under the influences of good and evil. That is what we are facing on earth. Too much evil about.

About sin and evil

How to destroy evil

If evil could be defeated our misery would be over. This idea strikes at the heart of what ideally should happen to our world. But how can evil be overcome? It originates from a spiritual force called sin, the most destructive power ever. Destroy sin and evil will disappear. This is only possible by another spiritual force defeating sin. That force must be totally opposite and more powerful. It is called love. Sin is so much ingrained in creation, that only a love as large as God's would suffice.

My friend was listening intently.

The plan

A fundamental confrontation

God decided to act. That always was the plan. A good God cannot but do otherwise. The spiritual power of love was to defeat that of sin in an all-out confrontation. Both love and sin are primary in our universe. So, the outcome of the battle would affect everything and be everlasting. All of creation would be delivered from the power of sin, if love were to be victorious. But how to make that happen? It would need something very special that only God could provide.

The battleground

The human person as the place

Spiritual forces manifest at many levels. From the animal world up to that ultimate level of moral intelligence. It was at this level that love and sin would face off. In the arena where both good and evil co-exist as a moral quality. The only place suitable for such a confrontation was within the human person. People are familiar with love and sin. So, God decided to become personified.

Christmas

The birth of the Son

If that sounds unbelievable, it must be remembered that there is a spirit connection between God and people. We are made in the image of God. The idea that God's Spirit might manifest as a person is not impossible. It would make that person born just as we are, but also of God. Such a man arrived as a baby Jesus in Bethlehem. His birth is remembered at Christmas.

The Cross

The power of sin defeated

In his early thirties, Jesus walked through Israel showing the love and power of God. The establishment hated him for it and he was crucified. While hanging on a cross, vulnerable and in agony, sin attacked in the form of its ultimate personification - Satan. Adding to Jesus' agony Satan threw all the destructive spiritual might of sin at Jesus Christ, who is the personification of divine love. It was a battle of suffering beyond imagination. In the end, love absorbed sin completely. It usurped all of its power. We have little idea what exactly happened. I wouldn't want to know. When the victory was complete, Jesus died.

Why sin?

We will not know

Why a good God allows such a situation to occur in the first place, is a good question. Could creation have come about without sin having a foothold? Apparently not. We will never find out why and simply must accept that. However much we may dislike it, our present reality is what it is. The Good News is that our misery will not be for ever. For surely, with such a high price paid by Christ for victory, a massive change may be expected.

My friend wondered whether this lets God off the hook too easily. I explained that God suffered as much as the Son Jesus. The battle involved divine love which can never be separated from God's reality.

Just imagine!

All the people very happy!

Just imagine a world without sin and suffering. Great happiness and no more death. Death occurs because of sin has infiltrated the fabric of creation. After Christ's victory a new world without sin became possible. It is our future.

That incredible day of Easter

Christ resurrected

It brings us to the pivotal point of the story. How can an existence without sin be known as real? By a new kind of being presenting itself. Jesus rose from the dead. He was unlike any person that ever existed. His followers met a new Jesus, unblemished and living forever. Sin and death no longer had a hold. This appearance of the resurrected Christ was the start of a new creation. Many will follow in this transformation. The arrival of the new Jesus is celebrated at Easter.

An additional spirit

Becoming born again

God resurrected Jesus with a spirit different from the one he was born with in Bethlehem. God is spirit and God creates. All of creation issues from spirit. Both the spiritual and the physical. After Christ's victory, God released an additional expression of spirit into our creation. Without changing its physical nature, as yet. Jesus foretold this in saying that believers would be born again. This time of a holy spirit. Not that a Christian has two spirits. The earthly and holy spirits are interwoven.

Eternal life

The best is yet to come

The new, holy spirit is eternal. A person born of it lives forever. Better still: after our natural death a wonderful, new existence lies ahead in heaven. That is why this story is called Good News.

Grace enablement
Improved spiritual ability

A believer in Jesus becomes especially enabled. It is called grace. It is an influence that helps you in coping with life. It just does, if you keep an awareness of Jesus at the back of your mind. You can have confidence in grace even though it may not seem obviously at work. The spiritual is always elusive.

The sin perspective
Liberation rather than accusation

One day the whole of creation will be changed into a new world. The process has already begun but is not noticeable. But people can enter into it by choice. The Bible talks about sinners. Everybody has sinned and doesn't measure up to God's standards. That simply is a statement of fact. It is not an accusation. It accepts that people are burdened by the influences of sin from birth. God does not hold anyone responsible for that. What I am responsible for is wilful wrongdoing. This moral scab on my life, and everyone has one, will have to disappear for me to enter the New Reality on offer. Christ came to liberate me. My choice is whether to enter into that liberation.

Forgiven!

What it means

God's message of love declares that all will be forgiven in Jesus. I activate my liberation by a step of faith. I say to God that I believe in the Good News and like to live in that way. My scab will be no more. I am forgiven. Not then to do whatever pleases, but to do my best in living well. Any mistakes I make will be forgiven when I owe up before the Lord honestly. My liberation remains complete. This is a spiritual reality. The same reality that underpins all of creation.

Why become a Christian?

A privileged life

Many theologians hold that because all of creation exists in Christ, it will be liberated freely and completely into a New Creation. That includes humanity, of course. Then, why become a Christian, you might ask. If heaven awaits anyway? It is a matter of opportunity. Following Jesus is a massive privilege. I may already now tap into the power of an eternal future. A power that will enrich my life greatly. My acceptance of Jesus brings many benefits. I become spiritually alert. Life increases in meaning. I know what I'm about and don't need society's approval. I am free in many ways and will follow the wisdom of Jesus. It offers the very best for wellbeing.

The door

An inescapable passage

Life in Christ is eternal. He is the door into our heavenly future. After death, everyone will meet up with his love when passing through that door. That love will reveal what a person is really like. There is an evaluation. Only true evil will have a grim time with that. Love will seek to open the door into heaven as much as possible.

Christians will enter heaven in a different way. They have already stepped through the door. A reward may be waiting, if they have made good of the privilege of being a believer. In case of dismal failure, in a very bad way without repentance, that person will suffer loss. It is for God to decide what that means. A God who is motivated by love and mercy.

The Choir

The benefits of church

Church is like a community choir. If you have a song in your heart, then that choir is a good place for learning to sing. You will soon figure out that it has some very good singers. But also mediocre and possibly false ones. Nothing is perfect in life.

In becoming a competent singer you must learn to read the score. Vocal chords need developing. You are asked to sing in harmony. Fit in with how the music is interpreted.

You may not like some of the songs. But you are there to learn. One day you will find, that you have a good musical understanding. Life has changed. With a song in your heart that will never cease. No matter where you are. All because once you joined the choir.

Why Christianity?

It solves the major problem best

The Good News bells the cat. Unlike other faiths, it faces the problem of sin head-on. It offers a solution that is a sure fact and fully accomplished. It also offers all the practices that are found so attractive in other religions. Like meditation and contemplation, in which Christianity has a rich tradition. While the Bible is second to none as sacred Scripture.

Above all, Jesus is personal and close. God is not at a distance. Jesus is a friend in the true sense of that word. A spiritual relationship that is very real. Other religions offers nothing like that. The way of Christ simply is an awesome way to live.

My friend was happy to hear me out.

Thank you for reading this book.

I hope, you found it interesting.

For more, see the next page.

Many blessings,

Michael

Books by Michael J Spyker
Available at agapedeum.com

Trilogy

Meeting Emma

A journey of discovery in which Emma becomes familiar with the many idea of Christian Spirituality through the ages. It helps her towards the person she would like to be. This book has assisted many in coming to love the vast wealth of the Christians spiritual tradition.

The Primacy of Love

Jake hears about his father's ideas on God's Love from Baz while travelling the Simpson Desert. Their talks include the significance of eternal and universal love, and the relational. The story has been called a significant theological feat.

The Language of Love

Emma and Jake fall in love. JH introduces them to the real meaning of Eros well beyond merely sex. They learn about being a Friend of Jesus and the language of love. Emma and Jake set off camping in the outback in search of JH. They work out what it means to live intimately together.

Novels

Julian's Windows

A musician and a teacher of children with intellectual ability fall in love. He lost his wife. She questions her vocation as a religious sister. Country life in Victoria restores his soul. A holiday in Australia from Liverpool decides her future. The ideas of Lady Julian of Norwich are an integral part of this love story in a most natural way. Great fun and informative.

Shalomat

Jacq and Ahmed, 16 years old, are on the run through Australia on a quest with mystical dimensions. It draws them together. All seems lost but isn't quite. Young people and adults enjoy this adventure. It is partly a comment on the one-sidedness of modern society and uses ideas of spirituality and philosophy. Will there be a sequel, an appreciative reader asked?

Treatise

Science and Spirit

Science exists by the creativity of God. But where to find God within physics? Where in society, in which God has become irrelevant? An informed answer best includes knowledge of history, science, philosophy, theology and religion. Plus ideas about a way forward. A read of significance to enjoy.

Christian Living

Drawings and Reflections

52 short reflections and 16 drawings that lift the spirit. A brief story that sows an idea. A picture to enjoy. It is not so easy to stay focused in a busy world. A little help always comes in handy. There is nothing religious about this book apart from keeping Jesus in mind and living vibrantly.

www.ingramcontent.com/pod-product-compliance
Lightning Source LLC
Chambersburg PA
CBHW071922130726
47909CB00014B/2531